EASY GUIDE

TO THE 20th CENTURY

Written by
Anne Peat

Illustrated by
Lorenzo Pieri
and Carlo Ferrantini

Kingfisher

CONTENTS

1900

1900: General Kitchener takes over British command in South Africa

1900: Sieges of Ladysmith and Mafeking, South Africa, relieved

1900: Boxer Rising begins in China

1901: Queen Victoria dies

1901: Social Revolutionary Party founded in Russia

1901: President McKinley assassinated, US

1902: Edward VII crowned after delay for an operation

1902: Treaty of Vereeniging ends Second Boer War in South Africa

1903: Social Democratic Party splits into Bolsheviks and Mensheviks in Russia

1903: Ford Motor Company founded

1904: Russo-Japanese War

Queen Victoria

In 1901, Queen Victoria died, aged 82. She had reigned for 64 years, longer than any other British monarch. Her son, Bertie, became King Edward VII, and succeeded her.

Second Boer War, 1899–1902

Boers fight British in South Africa
The Boer (Dutch) settlers were fighting for their independence. After their sieges of British settlements were broken, the Boers began a guerrilla campaign. Kitchener responded by burning their farms and imprisoning their families in concentration camps. **The Treaty of Vereeniging** in 1902, by which the Boer republics became part of British South Africa, ended the war.

Russia

At the beginning of the century, Russia was ruled by a Tsar. A movement for democratic reform started to grow.

Riots in 1902
Protests were led by students and workers.

The Boxer Rising, 1900

Kuang-Hsu   Tsu-Hsi

Leaders of The Boxers
The Boxers were a patriotic group in China devoted to martial arts. Their leader Kuang-Hsu, with the support of the Dowager Empress Tsu-Hsi, encouraged them to attack foreigners.

Teddy Roosevelt

After the shooting of McKinley in 1901, Theodore Roosevelt became the US President. His liberal ways, like inviting a black man to dine at the White House, angered some supporters.

Boxer soldiers
After Western missionaries were killed, troops were sent from Britain, the US, Germany, Italy and Japan to fight the Boxers and restore order.

Tientsin, 1900
The Allied troops took Tientsin after a fierce battle, and then relieved Peking (Beijing), where many foreign women and children were trapped in their Embassies.

Execution of Boxer leaders, 1901
The leaders of the rising were beheaded in public. The Chinese government had to agree to pay damages to the Allies, and allow Allied troops to stay in China.

Suffragettes in UK, 1903
In October 1903, The Women's Social and Political Union was formed in Britain to take militant action for votes for women. Its first leader was Emmeline Pankhurst.

Trans-Siberian railway, Russia
In January 1905, the Trans-Siberian railway was officially opened. Although not fully completed until 1917, it allowed swift travel across the Russian continent.

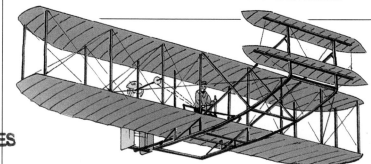

First powered flight, US, 1903
Wilbur and Orville Wright made the first powered flight in Kitty Hawk, North Carolina in 1903. Their flight lasted about a minute. They patented their 'flying machine', a biplane, in 1908. In 1909, Louis Bleriot flew from France to England in a monoplane, taking 43 minutes to cross the Channel. Also in 1909, the first international air race meeting was held at Rheims, France.

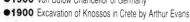

GALWAY COUNTY LIBRARIES

- **1900** Von Bulow Chancellor of Germany
- **1900** Excavation of Knossos in Crete by Arthur Evans
- **1901** Parliamentary Labour Party founded in UK
- **1901** Commonwealth of Australia established
- **1901** First Nobel Prizes awarded

- **1902** First Aswan Dam opened in Egypt
- **1902** Balfour becomes British PM
- **1902** US buys Panama Canal rights
- **1902** Anglo-Japanese alliance signed
- **1902** UK Education Act puts schools under local authority control

- **1903** First Tour de France cycle race held
- **1903** Revolution gives Panama independence
- **1903** First motor taxis appear in London
- **1903** Pius X is elected Pope

- **1904** British forces capture Lhasa, capital of Tibet
- **1904** Entente Cordiale signed between UK and France
- **1904** Drink licensing laws introduced in UK
- **1904** Non-violent picketing legalized during strikes in UK
- **1904** JM Barrie's *Peter Pan* first performed in London

Russo-Japanese War

Russian troops, 1904
The Russians and the Japanese fought for control of Manchuria (northern China) and Korea. The Japanese captured the Russian naval base at Port Arthur.

Russian fleet sunk, Tsushima, May 1905
After more Japanese victories, the Russian Baltic fleet was destroyed at Tsushima. The Russians signed the humiliating Treaty of Portsmouth, which ended the war.

Vladimir Ilyich Ulyanov (Lenin)
Although Lenin lived in exile, he was the leader of the Bolshevik section of the Social Democratic Party. His revolutionary ideas influenced both workers and students.

Bloody Sunday, 1905
In January 1905, the tsar's soldiers opened fire on demonstrators in St Petersburg. They killed and wounded hundreds of people, including women and children.

First duma (parliament), 1906
Peasant revolts, rioting, naval and army mutinies and a general strike followed the massacre. To restore peace, Tsar Nicholas II had to agree to elections for a duma.

Stolypin becomes premier, 1907
Unrest continued, forcing more concessions from the tsar. There were pogroms (attacks) against Jews. Stolypin became chief minister and began social and economic reforms.

Model T Ford, US, 1908
This was the first mass-market car. It was based on a standard model with interchangeable parts.

1905: **Sinn Fein founded, Ireland**

1906: **Suffragette protests in UK at opening of Parliament**

1906: **Indian Congress demands self-government**

1907: **Bill to enfranchise women in UK defeated**

Scouts and Guides
Robert Baden-Powell founded the Boy Scouts in Britain in 1907. The first Girl Guide troop was established in 1909 by his sister, Agnes.

1908: **Model T Ford goes into production in US**

1908: **Old Age Pensions Bill passed in UK**

Women's fashion
Skirts were long and ladies always wore hats and gloves outdoors, but during this decade dress became less elaborate. Tight corsets and bustles began to go out of fashion.

San Francisco earthquake, 1906
A massive earthquake in April 1906 destroyed most of the city. Business and industrial areas were damaged, and at least one thousand people were killed.

1909: **Union of South Africa proclaimed**

1909: **National Association for the Advancement of Colored People formed in US**

Robert Peary reaches North Pole, 1909
US Commander Robert Peary, and his black assistant, Matthew Hensen, reached the Pole on foot in April 1909.

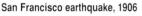

- **1905** Norway becomes independent from Sweden
- **1905** Heinz puts baked beans on sale in UK
- **1905** Zionist Congress calls for Jewish homeland in Palestine
- **1906** Launch of first British *Dreadnought* warship
- **1906** Amundsen determines magnetic North Pole
- **1907** New Zealand becomes a dominion
- **1907** Russia, France and Britain sign the Triple Entente
- **1908** Austria annexes Bosnia-Herzegovina
- **1908** Bakelite invented in US by LH Baekeland
- **1908** Earthquake in Calabria and Sicily, Italy. 150,000 killed
- **1909** Lloyd George's 'Peoples Budget' in UK
- **1909** First *kibbutz* founded in Degania Aleph, Palestine
- **1909** First colour movie shown in UK cinema
- **1909** Anglo-Persian Oil Company formed

1909

1910

1910: Two General Elections in Britain

1910: King Edward VII dies. George V becomes king

1911: Parliament Act limits power of Lords in UK

1911: China becomes a republic after Manchu emperor flees

Amundsen at the South Pole, 1911
The Norwegian explorer, Roald Amundsen reached the South Pole in December 1911. All the members of RF Scott's rival British expedition, which reached the Pole in January 1912, died on the way back.

Russian Revolutions

Kremlin, Moscow
The extravagance of the royal family, typified by their palaces, continued to arouse opposition. Premier Stolypin was assassinated in 1911 and more repression followed.

Rasputin
The tsarina came under the influence of a sinister monk, Rasputin who said he could cure her son of haemophilia. Rasputin was murdered by two nobles in 1916.

1912: War in the Balkans

1912: *Pravda* first distributed in Russia

1913: Coup d'état by the Young Turks in Turkey

1914: Gandhi returns to India from South Africa

1914: Archduke killed in Sarajevo by Serb

1912: Protests in Ulster against Irish Home Rule Bill

1914: World War I begins in Europe

Macchu Picchu
Hidden for 400 years, this Andean mountain fortress of the Inca empire was rediscovered by the American explorer, Hiram Bingham, in 1911.

Titanic sinks, 1912
When launched, this luxury liner was declared 'unsinkable' by its owners. On its first voyage across the Atlantic, it struck an iceberg and sank, with the loss of 1,500 lives.

Mexican Revolution

Pancho Villa
In 1911, US troops crossed the Rio Grande to support Mexico's President Diaz against the rebels led by Zapata and Pancho Villa. Diaz resigned and went into exile. However, civil war continued, and in 1916, US troops again entered Mexico to punish Villa for his raids into the US.

The Curies
In 1911, Marie Curie won a second Nobel Prize for her work on the new elements of radium and polonium. The first, in 1903, was shared with her husband, Pierre.

Woodrow Wilson 1912
Wilson, a Democrat, was elected US President in 1912. He took the US into World War I on the side of the Allies, and worked to establish the League of Nations.

Panama Canal opened, 1913
The canal was built to link the Pacific and Atlantic oceans. US President Wilson officially opened the canal by detonating an explosion from his White House desk.

Ireland

Home Rule Bill, 1912–13
Pressure for Irish independence by the Nationalists provoked the formation of the Unionist Party, which led opposition in Ulster and Parliament to Home Rule.

Easter Rising, 1916
Nationalists led by Pearse and Connolly launched a rising in Dublin. They took control of the General Post Office, fired on the castle and proclaimed an Irish republic.

British crush the rising
After British troops moved in, and the rebel strongholds were shelled by gunboats from the River Liffey, the rebel leaders were captured and the rising crushed.

● **1910** Russian Duma abolishes Finnish independence
● **1910** Union of South Africa becomes a dominion
● **1910** Revolution in Portugal overthrows king
● **1910** First labour exchange opens in UK
● **1910** Mexican Revolution begins
● **1911** Many strikes in UK
● **1911** Shops Act gives half-day off a week to workers in UK
● **1911** 40,000 march in London for 'Votes for Women'
● **1912** Morocco declared a French and Spanish protectorate
● **1912** SOS in Morse code adopted as distress signal
● **1912** Suffragettes arrested after protest at the House of Commons, London
● **1913** Second Balkan War begins
● **1913** Ulster Volunteer Force formed
● **1914** Egypt becomes a British protectorate
● **1914** Foundation of African National Congress (ANC)
● **1914** British explorer Besley discovers lost Inca cities in Peru

February Revolution, 1917
In February 1917, workers and soldiers rose in revolt in St Petersburg. The tsar failed to crush the revolt with Cossack troops, and was forced to abdicate.

October Revolution, 1917
A provisional government was formed. Lenin returned and, in October led a successful Bolshevik coup. He took Russia out of World War I, making peace with Germany.

Royal family murdered, 1918
The tsar and his family were sent into exile in Siberia. White Russian forces fought to free them. In 1918 the whole family were murdered in a cellar in Ekaterinburg.

Leon Trotsky
After playing a major role in organizing the October Revolution, Trotsky became a minister. As Commissar for War, he created the Red Army to fight the White Russians.

Cakewalk
Many new dances, like the Cakewalk, Grizzly Bear and the Turkey Trot, started in the US, then swept through Europe. They were very different from formal ballroom dances, and shocked older people.

1916: **Easter Rising of Nationalists in Dublin**

1917: **Balfour Declaration: British support for Jewish State**

Extent of Austro-Hungarian Empire, 1914

Emperor Franz Joseph
Before his death in 1916, Franz Joseph ruled a vast empire which stretched from Austria to the Balkans. World War I and nationalist movements broke up the empire, leaving Hungary, Austria and Czechoslovakia as independent republics.

China

Dr Sun Yat Sen
In 1911, a rising led by young idealists overthrew the Manchu dynasty. China became a republic, with Sun Yat Sen as president. He resigned in favour of Yuan Shih Kai in March 1912.

May the Fourth movement
A protest by Peking students against Japanese territorial aggression in May 1919, became a wider movement, which turned into the Chinese Communist Party in 1921.

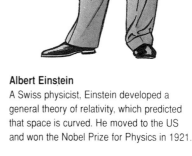

Albert Einstein
A Swiss physicist, Einstein developed a general theory of relativity, which predicted that space is curved. He moved to the US and won the Nobel Prize for Physics in 1921.

1917: **Revolutions in Russia establish Communist state**

1918: **Armistice ends World War I**

1919: **Treaty of Versailles**

Rebel Leaders executed
Fifteen leaders of the rebellion were shot. Sir Roger Casement, a British diplomat who arranged German support for the rebels was tried and hanged for treason.

Amritsar massacre, India 1919
During this decade Indians protested against the rule of the British Raj. Mohandas Gandhi returned from South Africa and became a leading protestor. In April 1919, Gurkha and Indian troops, commanded by Brigadier Dyer, opened fire on an unarmed crowd of Sikh demonstrators in Amritsar, North India, injuring 12,000 and killing 379. The India Act which followed granted limited self-rule to India.

- **1915** All-party coalition Government in UK
- **1916** Massacres of Armenians by Turks
- **1916** British Summer Time introduced
- **1916** Conscription introduced in UK
- **1916** Wolf Cubs formed in Britain
- **1917** Mata Hari executed as a spy in Paris
- **1917** British Royal family takes name of Windsor
- **1917** Nobel Peace Prize won by Red Cross
- **1917** Capital of Russia moved from Petrograd to Moscow
- **1918** Worldwide flu epidemic kills millions
- **1918** 'Khaki election' in UK won by Lloyd George
- **1919** Geneva chosen as meeting place of League of Nations
- **1919** Foundation of Communist Third International
- **1919** Sinn Fein organize independent *Dáil* (Parliament) in Ireland

1919

Balkan Wars, 1912–13

The Balkan League was formed by Greece, Serbia, Bulgaria and Montenegro; states which had won their independence from the Ottoman Empire (Turkey). In 1912, they fought the First Balkan War against Turkey to gain independence for more Slav territory in Europe. Turkey was defeated, and lost most of its European territory. Then members of the League fell out over which country should take the new territory. In the Second Balkan War in 1913, Bulgaria was stripped of its gains. The larger Serbia that resulted threatened Austro-Hungary with its claims on Croatia. Russia supported Serbia in its claims, and Germany supported Austro-Hungary. Thus, nationalist agitation in the Balkans resulted in confrontation between the two alliances of the Great Powers, and lead to war.

WORLD WAR I

In 1914, Europe was divided between two alliances of the Great Powers: the Triple Entente of Russia, France and Britain, and the Triple Alliance of Austro-Hungary, Germany and Italy. Each state was pledged to support its allies in war. Frequent disputes over territory, especially on the edges of the Austro-Hungarian Empire, led to the outbreak of a European war in August 1914, which spread to a large part of the world.

1914 Austro-Hungary declares war on Serbia; Germany declares war on Russia and invades Belgium

1914 Japan declares war on Germany and invades its Asian colonies

1914 Great Britain and France take German colonies in Africa

1914 British expeditionary force lands in France and fights at Mons

1914 Russians defeated by Germans at Tannenberg

1914 Russian victory at Lemberg

1914 British cruisers *Crecy, Hogue* and *Aboukir* sunk in North Sea

1914 Turkey attacks Russian ports on the Black Sea

1914 Four German battleships sunk off Falkland Islands by British Navy

1915 U-boat blockade begins

1915 Battle for Hill 60, Ypres

1916 Battle of the Verdun

1916 Battle of the Somme

1916 Conscription introduced in Great Britian for men aged 18 to 41

1916 US nationals join Allied air force. Germany protests

1916 Major naval battle off Jutland between British and German cruisers

1917 First US troops arrive in France. Draft introduced in US

1917 First great tank battle at Cambrai, France

1918 US President Wilson produces 14 point peace plan

1918 Russia withdraws from war. Germans launch a final offensive

1918 Germans pushed back to Hindenburg Line by British, American, Canadian, Australian and French troops

Archduke assassinated

In June 1914, the heir to the Austro-Hungarian throne, Archduke Franz Ferdinand, was shot in Sarajevo by a Serb nationalist. Austria threatened Serbia in retaliation, and Russia mobilized to protect Serbia. Germany feared invasion by Russia and France, so attacked France through Belgium. This brought the British Empire into the war, in support of Belgian neutrality.

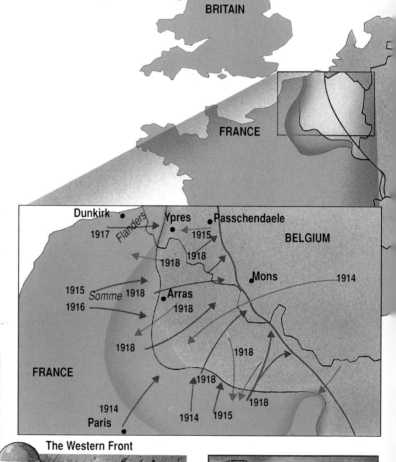

The Western Front

Trench warfare

Much of the war on the Western Front was fought between soldiers from lines of trenches. The attacking army climbed out of their trench and tried to capture the enemy trenches. Most were cut down by machine gun fire as they went 'over the top', and more drowned in the mud-filled shell holes and trenches. In the great battles of the war, such as the Somme, Verdun, Ypres and Passchendaele, thousands died on both sides to gain a few hundred metres of territory in Flanders.

Germans use gas warfare

The Germans used chlorine gas as a weapon from 1915. It blinded soldiers and destroyed their lungs. Gas masks provided some protection, but they made it difficult to see. Later, mustard gas was also used.

War at sea

The main sea battles were between the British and German fleets off the Falkland Islands in the South Atlantic and Jutland in northern Europe. German submarines called U-boats tried to blockade Britain with attacks on merchant shipping, causing American casualties. This helped bring the US into the war in 1917.

War in the air

The 'Great War' was the first in which aircraft played a part. At first, planes were used for scouting for the army. Later, some were equipped with machine guns to shoot down scouts and became the first fighter planes. The first real air battle was at Ypres in 1917. The Germans used Zeppelin airships to bomb Paris and Britain in 1914 and 1915, but these were slow and easily shot down by fighter planes. In 1916, they began to use bomber aircraft. Bombing caused 1,100 civilian casualties in England in this war.

Tanks

The first armoured vehicle with tracks was built in Britain in 1915. It was nicknamed 'Little Willie'. A larger version, 'Big Willie', was used by the British at the Battle of the Somme in 1916, but too few tanks were made to be very effective.

Riga
1917
Vilna
1914
1915
1914
1915
Warsaw
POLAND
1914
1916
1914
1918
1914
1916
RUSSIA
1914
1917
1915
1915
Vienna
1915
AUSTRIA-HUNGARY
1917
1916
1918
1916
1916
1918
1916
Belgrade
1916
Black Sea
1918
Bucharest
GERMANY
ITALY
Sarajevo
SERBIA
1915
1916
1916
1916
1916
1915
BULGARIA
1915

Held by Triple Alliance, Dec 1917
Major Triple Alliance offensives
Major Allied offensives
Armistice Lines, 1917-18
Furthest German advance

Dardanelles • Gallipoli
TURKEY
1915

ANZAC troops on Gallipoli, 1915

The Allies attacked Turkey in the Dardanelles, to help Russia. The landing of British, French, Australian and New Zealand (ANZAC) troops on Gallipoli was a disaster, which caused nearly 200,000 casualties.

Lawrence of Arabia

In 1917, the Arabs rose in revolt against Turkey, and Britain sent Empire troops to help them. Captain TE Lawrence gave tactical guidance to the Arab princes and helped free Palestine and Syria from Turkish rule.

Armistice, 1918

During 1918, many Germans were taken prisoner. Germany's allies, Turkey, Bulgaria and Austria, sued for peace. The Germans finally signed the armistice at Compiegne, France on November 11, 1918.

Treaty of Versailles, 1919

The treaty which ended the war with Germany was drawn up by Clemenceau of France, Wilson of the US and Lloyd George of Britain. It imposed harsh reparation payments and loss of territory on Germany, which resented its terms.

1920

US: The Roaring Twenties

1920: League of Nations meets in Paris and Geneva

Prohibition, 1920
The 18th Amendment to the US Constitution banned the manufacture and sale of alcohol. Illegal drinking clubs sprang up as a result.

Ku Klux Klan (KKK)
The KKK, revived in 1915 to 'defend' white Protestant supremacy against blacks, Jews, Catholics and foreigners, claimed a million members by 1923.

Hoover head of FBI, 1924
In 1924, J Edgar Hoover became the first head of the FBI, a federal detective force, set up to oppose the gangs who ran the illegal trade in alcohol and drinking clubs.

Post-war Germany

After the war, the kaiser abdicated and the Weimar Republic was established. It faced a major economic crisis and political opposition from left and right.

Collapse of currency
The war reparations of $33.5 million, which Germany had to pay, destroyed the German economy. The deutschmark was often devalued and became worthless by 1923.

India

Indian nationalism
Gandhi began a policy of non-cooperation with the British authorities (Raj), to press for self-rule. Imprisoned in 1922, he was released in 1924 because of poor health.

1920: In Ireland Black and Tan special constables enforce martial law

1920: Nazi Party formed in Germany

1922: Irish Free State formed from 26 southern counties

1922: Russia becomes Union of Soviet Socialist Republics (USSR)

1923: France and Belgium occupy the German Ruhr to enforce reparations

Communist Russia

Death of Lenin, 1924
After Lenin's death, Joseph Stalin became the most powerful man in the USSR. He expelled his rivals from the Communist Party, then exiled them.

1924: Ramsay MacDonald PM in first Labour government in UK

Hindu-Muslim riots, 1924
Gandhi preached non-violence. When there were riots between Hindus and Muslims in 1924, he went on a 21-day hunger strike as a penance for their violence.

Native Americans (Red Indians)
In June 1924, 10,000 Native Americans met in Sand Springs, Oklahoma, to discuss issues of concern to them: their land, health, education and the problems of living in the modern United States. Some states offered Native Americans citizenship as early as 1901. By the Snyder Act of 1924, all Native Americans were granted full citizenship, but few applied for the vote.

Tutankhamun's tomb, 1922
The discovery and excavation of this tomb, by Howard Carter and Lord Carnarvon, started a fashion for all things Egyptian. It was full of "wonderful things", including objects made of gold and inlaid with jewels.

The beginnings of Fascism

Mussolini's march on Rome, 1922
Mussolini declared himself 'Il Duce' (leader) of the Fascists in 1921. In October 1922, he seized power in Italy, after leading his followers in a march on Rome.

Hitler's Beer-Hall *Putsch*, 1923
In Germany, Adolf Hitler formed the National Socialist (Nazi) Party. In 1923, he made an unsuccessful attempt (*putsch*) to overthrow the Bavarian government.

Mein Kampf
Hitler was sentenced to 5 years in prison, but was paroled after a year. In prison, he wrote *Mein Kampf*, an autobiography which set out his racist and fascist views.

- **1920** Joan of Arc canonized
- **1920** Soviet Russia makes abortion legal
- **1920** Communist Party formed in Britain
- **1920** Britain given mandate to rule Palestine
- **1920** Bolshevik Red Army defeats White Russians
- **1921** Sinn Fein wins election for Southern Irish Parliament
- **1921** Reza Khan leads coup d'état in Persia
- **1921** Kingdom of Iraq established
- **1921** Over 1 million unemployed people in UK
- **1921** Rudolph Valentino stars in *The Sheik*
- **1922** Pius XI becomes Pope
- **1922** Conservatives win UK General Election
- **1922** Egypt becomes independent from Britain
- **1922** Britain aids emigration to Australia through Empire Settlement Act
- **1923** First 24 hour Grand Prix car race held at Le Mans, France
- **1923** Turkey becomes a republic under Mustapha Kemal
- **1924** Republican Calvin Coolidge elected US President
- **1924** First winter Olympics held in Chamonix

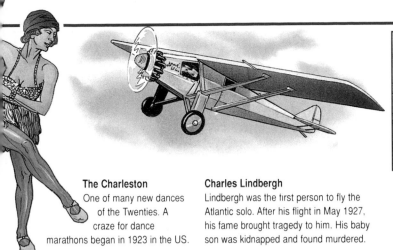

The Charleston
One of many new dances of the Twenties. A craze for dance marathons began in 1923 in the US.

Charles Lindbergh
Lindbergh was the first person to fly the Atlantic solo. After his flight in May 1927, his fame brought tragedy to him. His baby son was kidnapped and found murdered.

St Valentine's Day massacre, 1929
On February 14th, Mafia boss Al Capone's gangster mob, dressed as police officers, shot seven members of Bugsy Malone's rival gang near an illegal beerhouse in Chicago.

Wall Street Crash, 1929
The collapse of the New York Stock Exchange in October set off a worldwide economic crisis. Many investors lost everything; some even committed suicide.

Trotsky's downfall
In 1927, after Trotsky criticized Stalin, he was expelled from the Party, then sent into internal exile. In 1929, he was exiled from the USSR for anti-Soviet activities.

The General Strike, May 1926
Unemployment, and cuts in wages in mining and other industries, led to a nine-day strike in Britain. Volunteers kept essential services running, and the strikers were defeated.

Civil War in China

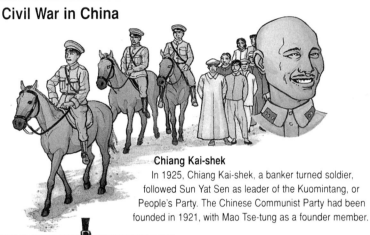

Chiang Kai-shek
In 1925, Chiang Kai-shek, a banker turned soldier, followed Sun Yat Sen as leader of the Kuomintang, or People's Party. The Chinese Communist Party had been founded in 1921, with Mao Tse-tung as a founder member.

1925: **Paul von Hindenburg becomes President of Germany**

1926: **Anti-British riots in Shanghai**

1927: **Inter-Allied control of Germany ends**

Baird invents television, London 1926
The first flickering pictures sent by television were of ventriloquist's dolls.

Hirohito, Emperor of Japan
Emperor Hirohito succeeded to the throne of Japan on the death of his father, Yoshihito, on December 25, 1926. His people regarded him as a god.

Civil war, 1925
Civil war flared up again in June 1925, after more anti-foreigner riots. Chiang Kai-shek used this as a chance to oppose the central government in Peking. At first, the Communists supported him. Chiang Kai-shek captured Shanghai and Peking and became President. Then he turned against the Communists, and cleared the Kuomintang forces of pro-Soviet elements.

Mussolini in power
Once in power, Mussolini banned other parties. The Socialist leader was murdered. After an election gave the Fascists 90 percent of the vote, Mussolini became dictator.

Lateran Treaty, 1929
Mussolini needed the support of the Roman Catholic Church. In the Lateran Treaty, he recognised the Vatican State, and made Catholicism the official religion of Italy.

1928: **Stalin's first five year plan in USSR**

1929: **Talks on Dominion status for India**

1929: **Second Labour government in UK**

1929: **Herbert Hoover becomes US President**

1929

● **1925** Cyprus becomes colony of British Empire
● **1925** Chrysler motor company founded in US
● **1925** Scopes trial over teaching evolution in Tennessee. US
● **1925** Boundary between Ulster and Irish Free State agreed
● **1925** George Bernard Shaw wins Nobel Prize for Literature
● **1926** Gertrude Ederle first woman to swim the Channel
● **1926** Empire prime ministers meet in London
● **1926** ICI chemical company founded in UK
● **1927** German stock market collapses
● **1927** First Volvo car manufactured in Sweden
● **1928** Britain gives vote to all women over 21
● **1928** Antonio Carmona becomes dictator of Portugal
● **1928** Kellogg Pact signatories renounce war
● **1929** Britain declares martial law in Palestine
● **1929** Academy awards (Oscars) established for cinema

1930

1930: Two million unemployed people in Britain

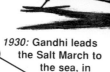
Amelia Earhart

The Depression

The collapse of the US stock market caused a worldwide crisis, leading to high unemployment and failure of businesses.

1930: Gandhi leads the Salt March to the sea, in India

Amy Johnson

1931: Japan seizes Manchuria

Women in the air

In April 1930, Amy Johnson became the first woman to fly solo to Australia from England. In 1932, Amelia Earhart became the first woman to fly solo across the Atlantic, from Newfoundland to Ireland. She disappeared in a flight across the Pacific in 1937 and no trace of her was ever found. She was assumed drowned when she crashed into the Thames in January 1941.

1932: Nazis take control of Reichstag (parliament)

1933: Hitler becomes Chancellor of Germany

Nazi Germany

The Reichstag burns, 1933

The Reichstag was destroyed by a fire soon after Hitler became Chancellor. The Nazis blamed the Communists for the fire, and then banned all other political parties.

Persecution in the USSR

Unemployment

People who had no jobs lived 'on the bread line'. They had to rely on unemployment benefit ('the dole' in Britain) and charity, to feed and clothe their families.

India

Salt March, 1930

Gandhi led a 320km march of poor people to the sea, where they made their own salt. This was to protest against the tax on salt levied by the British Raj.

1934: Pu Yi set up as puppet Emperor by Japan

1934: Night of the Long Knives in Germany

1934: Mao Tse-tung leads Long March in China

1935: Italy invades Abyssinia and uses poison gas

Dust bowl

In the US, a drought in the early 1930s made the effects of the Depression worse. Farmers and their families lost their homes and livelihoods as their crops failed.

Gandhi named Mahatma (Great Soul)

The British Raj imprisoned Gandhi for his campaign of civil disobedience. He went on hunger strike until he was released. Then he began a campaign for the rights of outcastes.

Sydney Harbour Bridge, Australia

When this opened in 1932, it had the world's longest steel arch and the widest carriageway of any bridge. It had tracks for trains and lanes for vehicles and cyclists.

Spanish Civil War

Franklin D Roosevelt

After Roosevelt became US President in 1933, he took action to beat the Depression, with work for the young unemployed and money for public works.

Jarrow March, 1936

There were marches in many countries to protest about unemployment. The 'Jarrow Crusade' was a march of unemployed shipyard workers from Jarrow to London.

Soup kitchens

Food for the unemployed and their families was provided in soup kitchens. Often, the food they got there was the only meal of the day for the very poorest people.

The Spanish Civil War, 1936–39

The war began when the Fascists, led by General Franco, challenged the left-wing Popular Front Government, using troops brought in by air from Morocco.

- **1930** First soccer World Cup won by Uruguay
- **1930** France begins to build the Maginot Line
- **1930** Jewish immigration to Palestine halted
- **1931** Pierre Laval becomes Premier of France
- **1931** King Alfonso leaves Spain after Republican victory
- **1932** Oswald Mosley forms British Union of Fascists
- **1932** Dáil in Irish Free State drops oath of loyalty to British king
- **1932** Famine in Soviet Russia
- **1932** Aldous Huxley's Brave New World published
- **1933** First traffic lights in Piccadilly, London
- **1933** Prohibition ends in United States
- **1933** Malcolm Campbell sets new land speed record
- **1934** Bonnie and Clyde, bank robbers, shot dead in US
- **1934** Liner Queen Mary launched in UK
- **1934** Driving tests introduced in Britain
- **1934** Sir Edward Elgar, composer, dies
- **1934** First recorded birth of quintuplets, Canada

SS Stormtroopers, 1934
During the 'Night of the Long Knives', Hitler's SS troops wiped out his rivals in the Nazi Party. He proclaimed himself Führer (leader) after Hindenburg's death in August.

Anti-Jewish Laws, 1935
The Nuremberg Laws allowed the Nazis to persecute Jews. Their shops were smashed, and they were forbidden to do certain jobs, marry non-Jews, or join the armed forces.

Luftwaffe formed, 1935
Hitler re-armed his nation in order to restore Germany as the Third Reich. A new air force, the Luftwaffe, was formed in 1935 to give the Nazis superiority in the air.

The Path to War

Mussolini and Hitler
In 1936, the two Fascist leaders established an alliance, the Rome-Berlin Axis. They supported other Fascist leaders in Europe against the democratic countries.

Persecution in the USSR, 1936
Stalin demanded that farms should operate as collectives; many peasants who objected were murdered. He also purged the Communist Party with show trials and executions.

Pu Yi and Mao's Long March, 1934
The Japanese siezed Manchuria from China and set up Pu Yi as their puppet emperor there. After his Communist forces were defeated by Chiang Kai-shek's Nationalists, Mao Tse-tung led them on a 9,700km 'Long March' to the safe province of Yenan. Two-thirds of his force died on the way.

Pu Yi

CHINA — Yenan — Junchin

China and Japan

Abdication, 1936
The British King, Edward VIII, gave up the throne to marry Mrs Simpson, an American divorcee. George VI and his wife, Elizabeth, became king and queen.

Edward VIII   Mrs Simpson

Munich Agreement, 1938
Hitler began to invade parts of other countries. At the Munich Conference, the British and French allowed him to annex part of Czechoslovakia, in a bid to avert war.

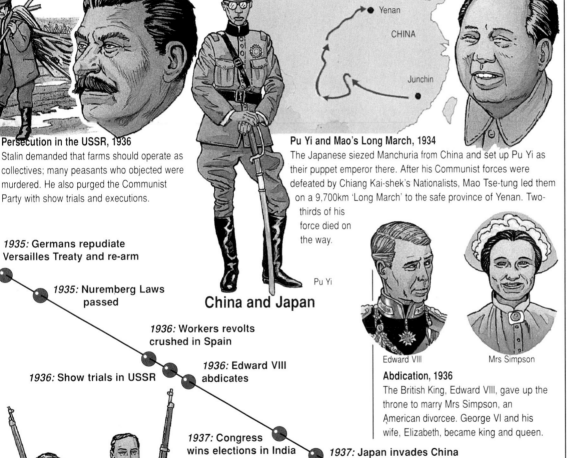

1935: Germans repudiate Versailles Treaty and re-arm

1935: **Nuremberg Laws passed**

1936: **Workers revolts crushed in Spain**

1936: Show trials in USSR

1936: **Edward VIII abdicates**

1937: **Congress wins elections in India**

1937: Japan invades China

1938: Japan bombs Shanghai and Canton

1938: **Munich Agreement**

1938: **Nazi Germany** *Anschluss* (union) **with Austria**

1938: **Germany annexes Sudetenland**

1939: **World War II begins**

International Brigade
Writers and idealists joined the 'International Brigade' to support the Government. Italy and Germany sent soldiers, bombers and weapons which helped Franco's Fascists win the war.

Hindenburg crash, 1937
Airships were a fashionable way to travel in the 1930s, but after the *Hindenburg* crashed in May 1937, killing 34 passengers and crew members, no more were made.

Invasion of Poland
After Hitler invaded Poland in September 1939, Britain and France declared war on Germany.

1939

WORLD WAR II
EUROPEAN THEATRE

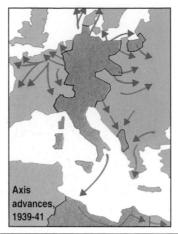

Axis
advances,
1939-41

When German SS units in Polish uniforms attacked a German radio station, this provided the pretext for the Nazi invasion of Poland on September 1, 1939. The UK and France declared war on Germany when it refused to withdraw. Australia and New Zealand also declared war, but the US and Italy remained neutral. A British force was sent to France, and French guns shelled Germany, but initially the main conflict was at sea.

German and Italian campaigns, 1939–41
After a *Blitzkrieg* (lightning-war) invasion by armoured divisions, German forces reached Warsaw. Poland fell, and was partitioned between Germany and the USSR. Germany tried to make peace with the UK and France, and the 'phoney war' followed. In March 1940, Italy agreed to fight with Germany against France and Britain. Germany attacked and occupied neutral Norway and Denmark, and Italy invaded British territory in North Africa, then Egypt, Albania, Greece and Romania. UK and ANZAC troops had initial success against the Italians in North Africa. Germany then attacked Malta and invaded Yugoslavia, Crete and Greece in 1941.

- **1939** August: German-Soviet non-aggression pact signed
- **1939** August: Children evacuated to the countryside from UK cities
- **1939** September: German U-boat sinks British liner *Athenia* on day war declared
- **1939** USSR invades Finland
- **1940** Italy declares war on Britain and France, June 10th
- **1940** France signs armistice and is partitioned. Marshal Pétain heads new Vichy government in southern France
- **1940** French fleet is destroyed by British to prevent Germans using it
- **1940** December: First British attack against Italians in North Africa
- **1941** German ship *Bismarck* sunk
- **1941** US destroyer *Greer* attacked by German submarine
- **1942** First US troops in Europe welcomed in UK. US bombers in action
- **1942** Raid on Dieppe by Allied troops tests invasion plans
- **1942** Allied victory at El Alamein
- **1943** US General Eisenhower takes command of Allied troops in North Africa
- **1943** Mussolini arrested. Italy declares war on Germany
- **1944** Failed Allied paratroop attack on bridges at Arnhem, Nijmegen and Grave
- **1944** Allies take Aachen
- **1944** October: UK troops land in Greece. Tito's partisans take Belgrade
- **1944** December: Field Marshal Von Rundstedt's last push in Ardennes, Belgium
- **1945** Dresden reduced to ruins by RAF and US air force bombers
- **1945** Allies liberate concentration camps at Belsen, Dachau, Buchenwald
- **1945** Germans surrender, May 7th. Victory in Europe (VE) Day celebrated, May 8th
- **1945** Collaborators Vichy (France) and Quisling (Norway) tried and shot
- **1946** Nazi leaders executed as war criminals after Nuremberg trials

Germany invades Low Countries, 1940
In May 1940, the Germans invaded Belgium, the Netherlands and Luxembourg. They pushed on into France after Belgium surrendered, and encircled the British and French army on the Channel coast.

Dunkirk, June 1940
An armada of 'little ships', ferries, fishing boats and river cruisers, sailed across the Channel to pick the Allied armies off the beaches at Dunkirk. 338,226 troops were rescued and brought safely back to the UK.

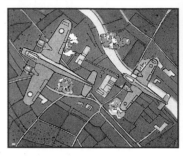

Battle of Britain, 1940
After the fall of France in the summer of 1940, Goering's Luftwaffe attacked British shipping and fought with the RAF over the Channel. His bombers attacked UK airfields and London, in preparation for an invasion.

Nazis invade USSR, 1941
In June 1941, Hitler broke his non-aggression pact with Stalin, and German panzer divisions stormed into the Ukraine. Advancing from the Baltic to the Black Sea, in three months they reached Moscow.

Campaign in North Africa, 1941–43
Rommel's *Afrika Korps* fought the Commonwealth 8th Army. Montgomery's 'Desert Rats' pursued them from El Alamein and, with Patton's US troops, encircled them in Tunisia in 1943.

The battle for Stalingrad, 1942
Late in 1942, the Germans fought for three months to capture Stalingrad. The Russians launched a counter-offensive and, by the end of January 1943, had surrounded the German 6th Army, which surrendered.

City bombings, 1940–45
The Germans began the Blitz on London in 1940. During 1941 the Luftwaffe attacked many UK cities. After 1942, the RAF and USAAF destroyed parts of Hamburg, Dresden, Cologne and Berlin with firebombs.

Allied troops land in Italy, 1943
From North Africa, the Allies invaded Sicily, and bombed Rome. The Italians surrendered. During 1944, the Allies fought the Germans through Italy and, after fierce fighting round Monte Cassino, took Rome.

D-Day landings, Normandy, France, 1944
On June 6, 1944 (D-Day), 176,000 British, Canadian and American troops fought to establish a beachhead in France. Fighting was fierce. The Americans on Omaha beach suffered 2,000 casualties that day.

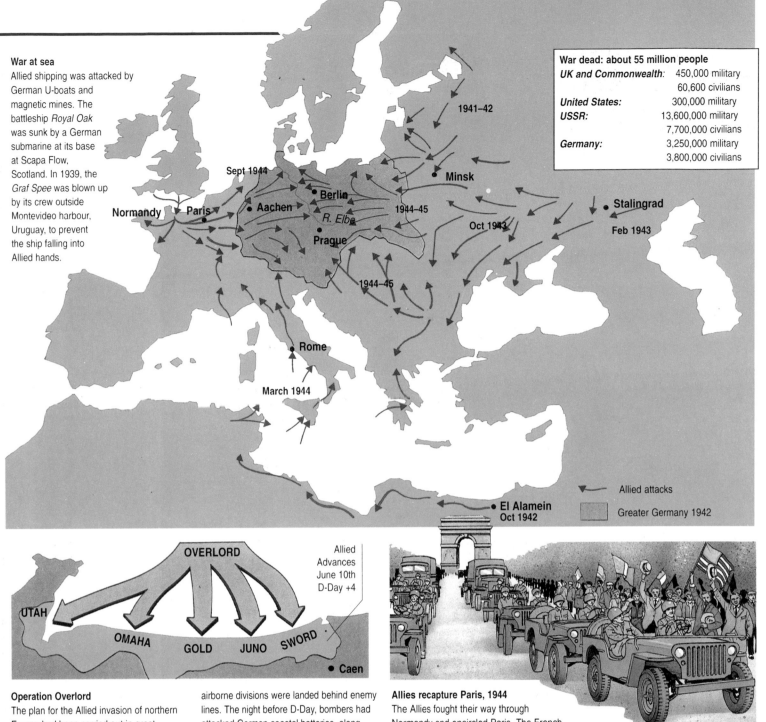

War at sea
Allied shipping was attacked by German U-boats and magnetic mines. The battleship *Royal Oak* was sunk by a German submarine at its base at Scapa Flow, Scotland. In 1939, the *Graf Spee* was blown up by its crew outside Montevideo harbour, Uruguay, to prevent the ship falling into Allied hands.

1941–42

Sept 1944

Normandy Paris Aachen Berlin Minst
R. Elbe 1944–45 Stalingrad
Prague Oct 1943 Feb 1943

1944–45

Rome

March 1944

El Alamein
Oct 1942

War dead: about 55 million people

UK and Commonwealth:	450,000	military
	60,600	civilians
United States:	300,000	military
USSR:	13,600,000	military
	7,700,000	civilians
Germany:	3,250,000	military
	3,800,000	civilians

Allied attacks
Greater Germany 1942

OVERLORD

Allied Advances June 10th D-Day +4

UTAH
OMAHA GOLD JUNO SWORD
Caen

Operation Overlord
The plan for the Allied invasion of northern Europe had been carried out in great secrecy and took the Germans in occupied France by surprise. Allied bombing destroyed railways and bridges, and three airborne divisions were landed behind enemy lines. The night before D-Day, bombers had attacked German coastal batteries, along with further bombardment from ships at sea. Four days after D-Day, the Allies had established a foothold in occupied France.

Allies recapture Paris, 1944
The Allies fought their way through Normandy and encircled Paris. The French Resistance rose against the Germans, and on June 25th, Free French forces under General De Gaulle entered the city. The German occupying forces disobeyed Hitler and surrendered.

V2 rockets
As the Allies pushed across Europe, Germany attacked London with V1 flying bombs and V2 long-range rockets with one-ton warheads. They were difficult to intercept, as they were fired from mobile launchers.

Rhine cities fall, 1945
The Allies tried to shorten the war by taking three Rhine bridges. Their attempts failed. The Germans counter-attacked in the Ardennes, but by March 1945, the Allies had crossed the Rhine and taken Cologne.

Berlin taken
The Soviet army pushed the Germans back through eastern Europe, and in April 1945 it captured Berlin. Hitler committed suicide as Russian troops approached his underground bunker.

Victorious leaders meet, July 1945
The meeting, at Potsdam, decided on the shape of post-war Europe and the frontiers of Germany. Conflict over Soviet support for Polish expansion into German territory ended the meeting in a mood of suspicion.

WORLD WAR II
PACIFIC THEATRE

Japan had been allied to Germany and Italy since 1936 and, in September 1940, joined the Axis powers pledging mutual economic and military aid. During the Sino-Japanese war, which began in 1937, British and American naval and merchant ships were attacked by the Japanese. The UK and the US protested against this and against Japanese expansion in Indochina. In 1941, they both froze Japanese assets.

USSR

MANCHURIA

CHINA

JAPAN

Midway

Pearl Harbo[r]

Okinawa

Iwo Jima

Hong Kong

FORMOSA

FRENCH
INDOCHINA

Luzon

Guam

PHILIPPINES

MALAYA

SINGAPORE

Pacific Ocean

BRUNEI
SARAWAK

JAVA

Java Sea

Guadalcanal

AUSTRALIA

Coral Sea

Japanese Empire and conquests to June 1942

Main Japanese attacks

Main Allied attacks

Extreme limit of Japanese advance 1942

War dead

Japan:	1,700,000	military
	350,000	civilians
China:	3,500,000	military
	10,000,000	civilians

Japanese expansion in China
Japan occupied large areas of China and set up a puppet government in Peking. In 1941, its forces occupied French colonies in Indochina and invaded Thailand, ignoring protests from the US, UK and Australia.

Attack on Pearl Harbor, 1941
Negotiations between Japan and the US to preserve peace broke down. On December 7th, Japanese planes bombed the US naval base at Pearl Harbor in Hawaii. They sank 19 ships of the Pacific Fleet, destroyed 200 aircraft and killed about 2,400 people. On the same day, Japan attacked US naval bases in the Philippines, Guam and Midway, and British bases in Malaya and Hong Kong. The Japanese declared war on the UK and US later that evening.

General Douglas MacArthur

In July 1941, MacArthur was appointed commander of US forces in the Far East, based in the Philippines. When the Japanese captured the islands in 1942, MacArthur withdrew to Australia vowing "I shall return".

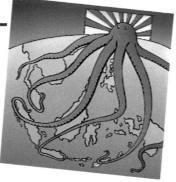

Japanese expansion

In December 1941, the Japanese took Hong Kong. They landed troops on the Malay peninsula, advancing north into Burma and south to Singapore. In 1942 they occupied Java, Borneo, New Guinea and Thailand.

Singapore falls, February 1942

The defence of Singapore was weakened by the sinking of the *Prince of Wales* and *Repulse*. The Japanese bombed the port and landed reinforcements. After weeks of heavy fighting, the garrison surrendered.

Battle of Midway, June 1942

The US fleet surprised the Japanese as they attacked Midway Island. After a four-day sea battle, in which American bombers sank three aircraft carriers, the Japanese fleet was forced to withdraw.

Japanese Prisoner of War (POW) camps

The Japanese despised troops who surrendered and treated prisoners with savagery. Civilian women and children were also marched long distances and interned in camps, where many died from starvation.

Philippines re-captured

In October 1944, MacArthur returned to the Philippines, landing at Leyte Gulf on Luzon. US naval superiority prevented Japan bringing in re-inforcements: In February 1945, Manila was taken and 5,000 prisoners were freed.

Battle for Iwo Jima, February 1945

The US lost 6,800 men, with 18,000 wounded to take this small island. It was captured to provide the base for fighters and bombers to attack the main islands of Japan. Most of the Japanese garrison died defending it.

Kamikaze pilots

As the tide of war turned against Japan, some of their pilots volunteered for suicide missions. Dressed in ceremonial uniform, and armed with impact bombs, they crashed their planes into the decks of enemy ships.

1937 British diplomat wounded when Japanese bomb Shanghai

1937 Japanese bombers attack UK and US vessels off China

1938 Japanese and Soviet troops clash in Mongolia

1939 Japan warns UK over its support for Chinese Nationalists

1940 Japanese invade Tonkin, a French possession in Indochina

1940 Japan warns UK against sending troops to Southeast Asia

1941 Australian troops sent to re-inforce Singapore garrison

1941 Tojo, who favours war with US, becomes Japanese PM

1941 Wavell made Commander-in-Chief of British, Dutch, Australian and US forces in South West Pacific

1942 Japanese capture 36,000 prisoners at Bataan. Many die on forced march to POW camps

1942 US planes bomb Tokyo

1942 Japanese bomb Ceylon

1942 Battle of Coral Sea

1942 US Marines land on Guadalcanal

1942 Australian and US troops fight Japanese in New Guinea

1942 Indian Army troops push Japanese back into Burma

1943 US takes Guadalcanal

1943 Japanese submarine torpedoes Australian hospital ship

1943 Auchinleck appointed Commander-in-Chief in India

1944 US attacks Guam and shells Japanese island of Paramishu

1944 Chindit troops landed by glider behind Japanese lines in Burma

1944 Guam retaken by US

1945 Allied supplies reach China via reopened Burma Road

1945 British 14th Army retakes Rangoon after three years

1945 Tojo executed for war crimes after failed suicide attempt

Okinawa, April 1945

American marines landed on Okinawa, imagining it to be lightly defended, but it took them three months to capture the island. Many Japanese leapt off the cliffs to their death rather than surrender.

Hiroshima, August 6, 1945

The US air force fire-bombed Tokyo and other Japanese cities. After the Japanese refused an Allied call to surrender, the newly developed atomic bomb was dropped on the city of Hiroshima.

Devastation

Virtually no buildings were left standing in Hiroshima, and 78,000 people were killed immediately. Many more died in agony in the following days, or contracted cancer years later as a result of exposure to radiation.

Japanese sign surrender document

The Japanese ignored an ultimatum, and a second atom bomb was dropped on Nagasaki. Then Emperor Hirohito ordered his troops to surrender. The document was signed on the USS *Missouri* on September 2, 1945.

1940

War on the home front

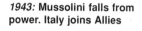

1940: Lascaux caves discovered, central France

1941: Germany invades USSR

1941: US enters World War II

1942: Gandhi imprisoned over demand that Britain leaves India

1943: Mussolini falls from power. Italy joins Allies

1943: German army surrenders at Stalingrad

1944: Ho Chi Minh declares Vietnam independent

1944: D-Day. Allied invasion of Normandy, France

1945: Labour government after British General Election

1945: Atomic bombs exploded at Hiroshima and Nagasaki

1945: World War II ends. Victory in Europe (VE) and Victory in Japan (VJ) celebrated

Rationing
In Britain and the US after 1941, some food, clothes and fuel were rationed by coupons. People had to queue for essential goods.

The Blitz
In British cities, people took refuge in air raid shelters and underground stations from Nazi bombing. Windows were covered with 'blackout' so no lights would show at night.

The Cold War

Churchill's 'iron curtain' speech, 1946
The USSR refused to allow free elections in the countries it occupied in East Europe. Winston Churchill said "an iron curtain has descended across the continent".

Jitterbug
The most popular wartime dance was the energetic Jitterbug. It started in the US in 1942, and spread to Europe with American wartime troops (GIs).

Lascaux cave paintings discovered, 1940
Prehistoric paintings, dating from about 20,000 BC, were discovered on the walls of the Lascaux caves in France. They showed animals and hunting scenes.

Occupation

The Holocaust
In German-occupied Europe from 1941, Jews were imprisoned, shot or deported to concentration camps, where millions were murdered in gas chambers by the SS.

Resistance movements
In Axis-occupied countries, ordinary people joined underground groups which carried out sabotage and helped Jews and other prisoners to escape.

Warsaw ghetto
The 100,000 Jews in the ghetto of Warsaw rose up against the Nazis in 1943. After the rising was crushed, the survivors were transported to concentration camps.

Independence for India

— Partition boundaries
— Disputed boundaries
● Predominantly Muslim
● Predominantly Hindu
○ Predominantly Buddhist

Concentration camps
Gypsies and other minority groups, as well as resistance fighters and opponents of the Nazis, were imprisoned, starved and killed in camps like Auschwitz and Dachau.

Forced labour, Burma railroad
Both Japan and Germany forced people from the countries they occupied to work for them. Many Allied soldiers died working on the Japanese military railway.

Refugees
Millions of men, women and children lost their homes and families in the war. When the fighting ended, they had to be fed, clothed and helped to settle in new homes.

Partition of India, 1947
India became two independent states, partiti on religious lines. India, led by Jawaharlal Nehru, was a Hindu state and Pakistan, led Mohammed Ali Jinnah, was Muslim.

- **1940** Churchill becomes British PM
- **1940** Home Guard created in Britain
- **1941** Commercial TV begins in US
- **1941** Churchill and Roosevelt sign Atlantic Charter
- **1941** Americans sign Lend Lease Act to help Allies
- **1942** Women called up in UK for work in factories and on farms
- **1942** Beveridge Report plans Welfare State in UK
- **1942** Foundation of Oxfam in UK
- **1943** Major polio epidemic in US
- **1943** Churchill and Roosevelt meet at Casablanca
- **1943** Musical *Oklahoma* popular in New York
- **1943** Gandhi protests in prison with hunger strike
- **1944** World Bank and International Monetary Fund set up
- **1944** German General Rommel commits suicide
- **1944** Red Cross wins Nobel Peace Prize
- **1944** July plot to kill Hitler fails
- **1944** Polish uprising in Warsaw crushed

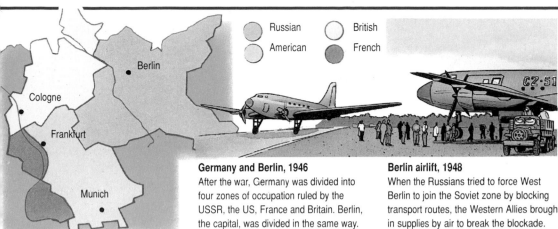

Germany and Berlin, 1946
After the war, Germany was divided into four zones of occupation ruled by the USSR, the US, France and Britain. Berlin, the capital, was divided in the same way.

Berlin airlift, 1948
When the Russians tried to force West Berlin to join the Soviet zone by blocking transport routes, the Western Allies brought in supplies by air to break the blockade.

Josep Broz Tito
In 1945, Marshal Tito, who had led the partisans against the Germans, formed a Communist government in Yugoslavia, which remained independent of the Soviet bloc.

Communist victory in Chinese civil war

Dior's 'New Look'
In 1947, French designer Christian Dior celebrated the end of wartime with his 'New Look'. Its long full skirts and tight waists brought back more feminine fashions.

Communist army
Mao's peasant army used the same guerilla tactics that had defeated the Japanese, to beat the Nationalist forces. In 1949, the Nationalists fled to the island of Taiwan.

Mao's victory
The Communists took Peking and proclaimed mainland China a People's Republic.

The United Nations

Charter signed, 1945
The UN Charter, setting up a new organization to promote international peace and security, was signed by delegates from 48 nations in San Francisco in June 1945.

Headquarters built, New York, 1946
The first meeting of the General Assembly, in London, chose a Norwegian, T Lie, to be General Secretary. In December 1946, New York became its permanent headquarters.

Palestine and Israel

UN Partition Plan, 1947
The arrival of Jewish refugees increased pressure for a Jewish state. A plan was produced to divide the land into two nations.

International zone
Jewish
Arab

EGYPT

Guerilla fighting
The British stopped Jewish immigration, and Jewish terrorist organizations attacked British targets. Arabs and Jews fought after the UN voted for a Jewish state.

Israel 1948
The British mandate ended, and the Jews proclaimed the state of Israel. War began as Arab states attacked the new nation.

Timeline:
- *1946:* Churchill's 'iron curtain' speech
- *1946:* First meetings of the United Nations General Assembly
- *1947:* Dior launches 'New Look' fashions
- *1947:* India, Pakistan and Burma independent
- *1948:* State of Israel proclaimed. Arab-Israeli War
- *1948:* Berlin airlift begins
- *1949:* USSR tests atomic bomb
- *1949:* North Atlantic Treaty Organization (NATO) set up
- *1949:* West and East Germany formed

Riots and massacres
Nearly half a million people were killed as refugees escaped to the country of their religion. The assassination of Gandhi in 1948 sparked off more rioting.

De Havilland *Comet*, 1949
In July 1949, the world's first jet airliner made its maiden flight at Hatfield, England. It made its first scheduled passenger flight to Johannesburg in May, 1952.

1949

- ●**1945** Mussolini shot by Italian partisans
- ●**1945** Harry Truman becomes US President
- ●**1945** US night bombing of Japanese cities
- ●**1945** Churchill, Roosevelt and Stalin meet at Yalta
- ●**1945** Stalin, Attlee and Truman meet at Potsdam
- ●**1946** De Gaulle resigns as French President
- ●**1946** London Airport opens at Heathrow
- ●**1947** Britain raises school leaving age to 15
- ●**1947** Lord Mountbatten appointed last Viceroy of India
- ●**1947** US Marshall Aid plan for Europe
- ●**1948** National Health Service begins in UK
- ●**1948** Apartheid begins in South Africa
- ●**1948** World Health Organization founded
- ●**1949** Clothes rationing ends in UK
- ●**1949** George Orwell's *1984* published
- ●**1949** Eire leaves the British Commonwealth
- ●**1949** Soviets test their first nuclear bomb

1950

Cold War suspicion

1950: McCarthy allegations begin in the US

1951: Conservatives win UK General Election

1952: Eisenhower elected President in the US

The way we lived

Technological advances, many of them developed in wartime, changed everyday life for ordinary people in the West.

Telephones
Telephone ownership soared in the US and Europe, and advances such as the transatlantic cable meant that families could keep in touch across the world.

Television
During this decade, television began to replace radio as the major home entertainment. Britain's first commercial channel (ITV) began broadcasts in 1955.

Hula-hoops, 1959
Hula-hoops were one of many short-lived leisure crazes which swept post-war Europe and America. Manufacturers promoted them through TV and magazines.

McCarthy witch hunts
Fear of the USSR was behind Senator Joe McCarthy's campaign to expose Communists in the US media and government. From 1953 he did this through the Senate Permanent Sub-committee on Investigations, of which he was the chairman.

Korean War, 1950–53
Korea was divided along the 38th parallel between the Communist North and the South. When North Korea invaded the South, a three-year war began, which drew mainly American, UN and Chinese troops into the fighting. At the end of the war, the border was unchanged.

1952: **King Farouk of Egypt overthrown**

1952: **State of emergency in Kenya over Mau Mau**

1952: **European Coal and Steel Community formed**

1953: **End of Korean War**

1954: **Algerians begin revolt for independence from France**

Four-minute mile, 1954
In 1954, in Oxford, England, Roger Bannister set a new world record, and became the first person to run a mile in under four minutes.

1954: **End of food rationing in UK**

Coronation of Elizabeth II, 1953
Elizabeth came to the throne on the death of her father, King George VI. The the young queen was crowned in June 1953, in the first royal occasion to be televised.

Atomic arms race
In 1951, the US exploded the first Hydrogen bomb. By 1957, the USSR and Britain also had H-bombs, and there was worldwide fear of a nuclear world war.

'Ban the Bomb' demonstrations
Eminent scientists, like Linus Pauling, warned of the genetic dangers of nuclear tests. Protest movements, like CND in Britain, marched and demonstrated for disarmament.

Conquest of Mount Everest, 1953
New Zealander Edmund Hillary and a Nepali Sherpa, Tenzing Norgay, became the first people to climb the world's highest mountain, on May 29, 1953.

Nasser takes power in Egypt, 1953
Colonel Nasser led the 'Free Officers' who overthrew King Farouk of Egypt. In 1956, Nasser took control of the Suez Canal Company away from the British and French.

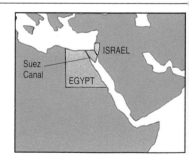

The Suez Crisis, 1956
Britain thought that control of the canal was vital for its trade with its Empire. With France and Israel, Britain invaded Egypt. Port Said and Cairo were bombed from the air.

- ●**1950** O' and A' level exams introduced in England and Wales
- ●**1950** First British national park designated
- ●**1950** Jordan annexes Palestinian West Bank
- ●**1950** Miners strike in UK
- ●**1950** Diners Club, first credit card issued
- ●**1951** Festival of Britain
- ●**1951** King Abdullah of Jordan assassinated
- ●**1951** Leopold of Belgium abdicates. Baudouin becomes king
- ●**1951** Coventry Cathedral designed by Basil Spence
- ●**1952** Linear B script deciphered by Michael Ventris
- ●**1952** Hussein becomes King of Jordan
- ●**1952** Ancient city of Jericho excavated
- ●**1953** Stiletto heels come into fashion
- ●**1953** Polio vaccine successfully tested
- ●**1954** US Supreme Court declares colour segregation in schools illegal
- ●**1954** SEATO formed to defend Western interests in Asia
- ●**1954** Billy Graham's evangelical crusades begin

Warsaw Pact, 1955
In 1955, the USSR formed a military alliance with seven of its Communist satellites in Eastern Europe, in opposition to the Western military alliance, NATO.

Nikita Khrushchev
After Stalin's death in 1953, Khruschev became the leader of the USSR. He visited the West, and tried to improve relations, but crushed risings in the Eastern Bloc states.

Hungary, 1956
Anti-Communist risings in Eastern Europe were crushed with Warsaw Pact troops. Twenty thousand people died during the Hungarian rising in November, 1956.

Cuba, 1959
In 1959, after a guerilla campaign against the dictator Fulgencio Battista, Fidel Castro took power on the island of Cuba, and established a Communist state in the Caribbean.

Racial tension in the US

Bus boycott in Alabama, 1955
A black boycott of buses in Montgomery, Alabama began after Rosa Parks defied a local law requiring her to stand at the back even when the seats for whites were empty.

The Rev. Martin Luther King Jr.
After King was convicted of organizing the boycott, he vowed to continue the fight for integration and black rights, using "the weapons of love and passive resistance".

Little Rock, Arkansas, 1957
In 1957, President Eisenhower sent Federal troops to ensure that black students could enter the High School in Little Rock, in accordance with Federal law.

Tibet

Chinese invasion, 1950
In 1950, Communist China invaded and conquered Tibet. The Chinese occupiers promised religious freedom to Buddhist Tibetans provided they cut ties with the West.

Tibetan uprising, 1959
In 1959, Tibetan nationalists rose against the Chinese, demanding that their independence be restored. The Chinese suppressed the revolt with great brutality, and the Dalai Lama, spiritual leader of Tibetan Buddhists, fled into exile in India.

1955: **Austria regains independence**

1955: **South Africa leaves UN over apartheid**

1955: **Britain declares state of emergency in Cyprus**

1956: **Khruschev denounces Stalin's policies**

1957: **Six European countries sign Treaty of Rome to form Common Market**

1957: **Harold Macmillan becomes British PM**

Elvis Presley was the greatest American star of the new rock-'n'-roll dance and pop music craze.

Buddy Holly
Though he was killed in a plane crash in 1959, Buddy Holly's records stayed popular, and influenced the British 'Mersey Beat' of the 1960s.

1956: **War between Israel and Arabs**

Anglo-French invasion of Suez
The invasion was condemned by the US and USSR, and the UN imposed a ceasefire. British and French troops withdrew, but the Israelis held on to land they won in Gaza.

General De Gaulle
De Gaulle, leader of the Free French in World War II, returned from retirement to rule France. His main task was to negotiate France's withdrawal from their colony in Algeria.

1957: **Ghana gains independence from Britain**

1958: **'Papa Doc' Duvalier becomes dictator in Haiti**

1958: **NASA established in US to plan space exploration**

1958: **De Gaulle elected President of France**

1959: **US troops sent to Laos**

1959: **Lunik III photographs Moon**

1959: **US Vice President Richard Nixon visits Khruschev in Moscow**

1959: **Stockholm Convention sets up European Free Trade Area**

1959

- ●**1955** Winston Churchill resigns as UK PM
- ●**1955** Disneyland opens in California, US
- ●**1955** Juan Peron overthrown in Argentina
- ●**1955** Hugh Gaitskell becomes leader of British Labour Party
- ●**1955** Duke of Edinburgh starts his award scheme for young people
- ●**1956** Wimpey brings first hamburger restaurants to Europe
- ●**1956** Self-service shops appear in UK
- ●**1956** Petrol rationing in UK and France because of Suez crisis
- ●**1957** State of emergency in Eire after IRA bombing campaign
- ●**1957** Ancient Assyrian city of Nimrud excavated
- ●**1958** Race riots in Notting Hill, London
- ●**1958** Munich air crash kills members of Manchester United football team
- ●**1958** John XXIII elected Pope and begins reforms of Roman Catholic church
- ●**1959** Remains of Nutcracker man found in Tanganyika
- ●**1959** Alaska and Hawaii become 49th and 50th states of US

VOTES FOR WOMEN

The movement for women's suffrage (the right to vote) intensified in the US and the UK during the 19th century. A women's rights convention met in Seneca Falls, New York, in 1848 and two women's suffrage associations were formed by Susan Anthony, Elizabeth Cady Stanton and Lucy Stone in 1869. Beginning with Wyoming in 1890, various states gave the vote to women in state elections. In the UK, a women's suffrage committee was formed in Manchester in 1865. Women taxpayers could vote in local elections and sit on some local councils from 1869.

WSPU founded in UK, 1903
Frustrated at the lack of progress in securing the parliamentary vote, Emmeline Pankhurst and her daughter Christabel formed the breakaway Women's Social and Political Union, to take more militant action.

Demonstrations
WSPU members, known as suffragettes, organized vast demonstrations, chained themselves to railings and damaged property. They were often attacked by opponents of women's right to vote.

Arrests and prison
In 1906, Sylvia and Adela Pankhurst were imprisoned, after refusing to pay fines for disrupting the opening of Parliament. More protesters were arrested after police used mounted charges to break up their marches.

Hunger strikes
As a protest against their imprisonment, many suffragettes went on hunger strike. The prison authorities responded by force-feeding them, pouring liquid through tubes down their throats and noses.

- **1905** Women's Suffrage Bill rejected by UK Parliament
- **1906** Women able to vote in New Zealand (1893) Australia (1902) and Finland (1906)
- **1906** UK suffragettes join suffragists in rally in New York
- **1907** First women elected to Parliament in Finland
- **1908** Elizabeth Garrett Anderson, UK's first female mayor
- **1913** UK suffragette Emily Davidson killed by racehorse in Derby Day protest
- **1914** Women's suffrage amendment rejected by US Congress
- **1915–19** Votes for women in Denmark, Norway, Russia, Germany, Poland and France
- **1916** Jeanette Rankin, first woman elected to US Congress
- **1928** Votes for all women over 21 in UK
- **1929** Margaret Bondfield, first woman in UK Cabinet
- **1969** Golda Meir becomes Prime Minister of Israel
- **1979** Margaret Thatcher first woman PM of UK
- **1980** Vigdis Finbogadottir premier of Iceland
- **1993** Women lead governments in Canada and Turkey

'Cat and Mouse Act', April 1913
After a campaign of window-smashing in the UK, many suffragettes were imprisoned. Because of concern over force-feeding, an Act was passed which allowed hunger-strikers to be released, then re-imprisoned when they were well again.

Washington march, 1913
In the US, suffragists were initially more peaceful. In March 1913, 5,000 women marched to the Capitol to speak to President-elect Woodrow Wilson about voting rights. They carried banners saying 'Tell your troubles to Woodrow'. Rowdy opponents attacked the marchers, causing a riot.

Lady Astor, MP 1919
In the World War I, women worked to support the British war effort, and public opinion became sympathetic to women's suffrage. Women over 30 were given the vote in 1918. In 1919, American-born Lady Nancy Astor became the first woman MP to sit in the British Parliament.

Frances Perkins, US Labor Secretary, 1933
The role played by women in the war swung Congress behind the suffragists, and national suffrage for women was given by the 19th Amendment in 1920. Frances Perkins was the first female Cabinet member in the US.

Mrs Sirimavo Bandaranaike, 1960
Worldwide, women could vote in more than 100 states. But by 1966 there were few women in positions of power. Mrs Bandaranaike became the first woman Prime Minister in the world, when she replaced her assassinated husband in Ceylon (Sri Lanka) in 1960.

FASHION

At the beginning of the century, only rich people, who could afford to have new clothes made for them, followed high fashion. The invention of new fabrics and techniques of mass manufacture meant fashion became cheaper and available to everyone by the second half of the century. Changes in fashion became more frequent and people wore a variety of styles.

1910 outdoor wear
During the first decade, women's clothes became looser fitting, and necks and ankles began to be daringly visible.

1913
Men often dressed formally, in top hat, gloves and waistcoat. Women's hobble skirts were difficult to walk in.

1920s flapper
After World War I, a boyish look was fashionable for women – hair was cut short and covered by cloche hats, and chest-flattening bras gave women a slim figure. Skirt lengths went above the knee.

- **1902** Sew-on press studs for clothing invented in France
- **1905** Viscose, an artificial silk, made by Courtaulds in UK
- **1909** First permanent waves offered by London hairdressers
- **1909** Italian Mariano Fortuny introduces silk pleating process for dresses
- **1913** Modern zip fastener developed in Sweden
- **1914** First bra patented in USA
- **1916** Rayon knitwear on sale
- **1916** French designer Coco Chanel promotes jersey as a fashion fabric
- **1925** Chanel's first collarless jacket
- **1925** In Paris, fashion designer Vionnet begins to use the bias cut
- **1927** Beards and moustaches go out of fashion for men in Europe
- **1932** Patent for crease-resistant process for fabric in UK
- **1933** Actress Marlene Dietrich sets trend for women wearing men's clothes
- **1934** Y-fronts introduced in men's underwear
- **1939** Nylon stockings first on sale in US
- **1941** Sale of silk stockings banned in UK during the war
- **1942** The first zoot suit produced in the US
- **1946** The bikini goes on sale
- **1948** Velcro fastening invented
- **1950** Terylene fabric on sale
- **1953** Stiletto heels for women's shoes appear
- **1954** Teddy boy look for youths
- **1954** Crew cut fashion in US
- **1954** Brando sets a fashion for denim jeans in film *The Wild One*
- **1958** Lycra elastic fabric patent
- **1970s** Punk fashion: chains, safety pins, pierced noses, torn jeans.
- **1988** Return of the miniskirt in clinging lycra fabrics

1930s
Tweed suits were in fashion for both men and women. Knickerbockers, for a sporty look, were popular with men. For women the clothes were long and lean.

1930s evening wear
Dresses became more feminine. Designers like Eva Schiaparelli used new fabrics like rayon and viscose, cut on the bias to hug the hips and flare out at the ankles. Many were backless, which was thought shocking.

1940s demob suit
During the war, men's suits were single breasted, and had no turn-ups or pocket flaps, to save fabric. UK servicemen were given a 'demob' suit, with a tie, socks, hat and pair of shoes, when they were discharged.

1940s wartime for women
Suits had square shoulders – the military look. Clothes had to be hard wearing and adaptable. Women wore their hair in tightly curled bangs (like sausages), to keep it neat while they did war work in factories.

1950s women's 'New Look'
The end of clothes rationing heralded a new, elegant look, the Dior 'A-line'. This emphasised the bust, waist and ankles. Hats and shoes completed the look. Underwear was important for giving women's figures the right shape.

1960s miniskirt
The 60s brought back a boyish look for girls and the shortest (mini) skirts ever – 25 centimetres above the knee. Patterned tights replaced stockings. Dresses in Op art designs were made from leather and plastic.

Flower power
Young people who 'dropped out' (rejected the values of society) in the late 60s and 70s wore kaftans, beads, flowers and long hair.

Labels
In the 80s and 90s, fabrics that had been used for casual wear, like denim and Lycra, were used for clothing that was considered stylish – especially if it had a 'designer' label on the outside.

1960

The Cold War

Rivalry between the superpowers, the USSR and the US, continued in the 1960s. There was a real fear that this would trigger a nuclear war which might destroy the planet.

1960: Cyprus and Nigeria become independent

1960: Civil War begins in independent Belgian Congo

1961: India seizes colony of Goa from Portugal

1961: Yuri Gagarin first man in space

1963: Nuclear Test Ban treaty signed by US, UK and USSR

U2 spyplane shot down, 1960
The USSR and the US spied on each other's weapons, bases and war plans. In 1960, the USSR shot down an American U2 spy-plane, and captured its pilot, Gary Powers.

Berlin Wall built, 1961
To prevent East Germans from escaping to the West through Berlin, a wall was built across the city by the Communists. Many people were shot as they tried to cross it.

1963: Sir Alec Douglas-Home becomes British PM

1963: Lyndon B Johnson becomes US President

1963: Crisis in Cyprus. UN troops deployed

1964: Labour wins UK election. Harold Wilson PM

1964: China explodes atomic bomb

1964: Malta, Malawi, Zambia become independent

1964: Civil Rights Act bans racialism in US

1964: Kosygin and Brezhnev replace Kruschev in USSR

South Africa

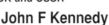

Sharpeville massacre, 1960
Black Africans demonstrated against the apartheid rules, which denied them equal rights. Police fired on demonstrators at Sharpeville and killed over 50 of them.

Mandela imprisoned, 1962
After worldwide protests, South Africa left the Commonwealth. It was banned from the Olympics in 1964. Black leaders, like Nelson Mandela, were imprisoned for treason.

John F Kennedy

President, 1961
The election of Kennedy brought an image of youth, glamour and culture to the White House. He was the first Roman Catholic President, and his programme promised liberal reforms at home and more civil rights for the people.

Kennedy assassinated, 1963
Kennedy was shot during a visit to Dallas in November 1963, by Lee Harvey Oswald. His brother, Robert, was also assassinated while campaigning to be President in 1968.

China

Mao's Cultural Revolution, 1966–69
China split with the USSR in the early 60s, claiming the Soviets had betrayed communism. Mao launched a Cultural Revolution to purify his party. Young Red Guards attacked anyone who represented tradition, including writers, bureaucrats, artists and teachers. Thousands were killed and imprisoned and the country was plunged into turmoil.

Black power in the US

James Meredith
Desegregation in the southern states brought violent protests by some whites. In 1962, when Meredith entered the University of Mississippi, 750 US marshals escorted him.

'I have a dream' speech, 1963
Dr Martin Luther King led the peaceful struggle for black civil rights. His speech spoke of his dream of equal freedom for all. In 1968, he was shot dead in Memphis.

Watts Riots, 1965
Riots flared in the black areas of US cities in the summers of 1965, 1966 and 1967. More riots followed the killing of Dr Luther King, as blacks despaired of non-violence.

Black power
Many blacks turned to more militant groups like the Black Panthers, and the Black Muslim movement, led by Malcolm X. Support for them was shown to the world when winning US athletes gave black power salutes at the Mexico Olympics in 1968.

- ●**1960** *Lady Chatterley's Lover* book trial in UK
- ●**1960** Harold Macmillan's 'Wind of Change' speech
- ●**1960** Olympic Games in Rome
- ●**1960** First contraceptive pills on sale in US
- ●**1960** *New English Bible* published ●**1961** Kuwait, Tanganyika, Sierra Leone independent
- ●**1962** Beatles first hit, *Love Me Do*. Start of 'Mersey Beat' pop sound
- ●**1962** Vatican II opens in Rome; begins reforms of Roman Catholic Church
- ●**1962** Jamaica, Trinidad and Tobago, Uganda independent
- ●**1962** Brazil wins the soccer World Cup
- ●**1963** Pope Paul VI elected
- ●**1963** Kenya and Zanzibar independent
- ●**1963** The Great Train Robbery in UK
- ●**1963** Profumo scandal rocks Conservative government in UK
- ●**1964** Warren Report on Kennedy assassination published
- ●**1964** Olympic Games in Tokyo
- ●**1964** Zambia becomes independent from UK
- ●**1964** Yasser Arafat leader of Palestinians

Bay of Pigs Invasion, 1961
The United States felt threatened by Castro's Communist regime in Cuba. The US backed an unsuccessful attempt by pro-Western Cuban exiles to invade and overthrow Castro.

Cuban missile crisis, 1962
'Spy' photographs showed Russian missiles, which could destroy US cities, being shipped to Cuba. With the world on the brink of war, the Soviets agreed to remove them.

Vietnam War

US troops in Vietnam, 1965
When the Soviet-backed North (Vietcong) invaded South Vietnam, US troops intervened. They bombed northern villages and used napalm to clear forests that hid the Vietcong.

Anti-war demonstrations, 1969
TV pictures of the effects of the war on Vietnamese peasants, and the number of US casualties, prompted protests against the war. 'Draft dodgers' refused to serve in forces there.

Swinging Sixties

Fashion and freedom
There was a fashion explosion in the 1960s. Cheap, exciting designs became easily available in small shops called boutiques. The miniskirt was the look for girls, with short straight hair, leather boots and pale lipstick. Men wore coloured shirts, wide ties and grew their hair long.

The Beatles and the 'pop revolution'
The Beatles, four lads from Liverpool, dominated the pop world in the 1960s. Their style changed from simple songs to complicated music using electronic effects.

Woodstock open-air festival, 1969
Pop festivals, like that at Woodstock, New York, attracted huge crowds of young people. These events promoted love and peace, but violence broke out at some festivals.

Independence

Algeria
In the 1960s, many countries gained their independence from European colonial powers. Algeria won freedom from France in 1962, after a violent eight-year guerilla war.

966: South African President erwoerd shot. Vorster ecomes President

Six-Day War, 1967
When the Arabs blockaded Israeli shipping, Israel launched a successful six-day campaign. They gained territory in Jerusalem, Sinai, the Golan Heights and the West Bank.

The 'Prague Spring' crushed, 1968
A more democratic reforming government in Czechoslovakia, led by Alexander Dubcek, was removed after Soviet tanks moved into Prague to prevent any change.

Jomo Kenyatta
The first leaders of the new nations were often former freedom-fighters. Kenyatta, President of Kenya, had been imprisoned for Mau-Mau activities by the British in 1952.

1968: Tet offensive by North on South Vietnam

Moon Walk, July 1969
American astronaut, Neil Armstrong, became the first person to walk on the Moon. He flew there in *Apollo 11* with Michael Collins and Buzz Aldrin.

1968: Vietnam peace talks open in Paris

1968: Abortion legalized in UK

1968: Palestinians hijack Israeli aircraft

1969: Golda Meir becomes Israeli PM

1969: Nixon becomes US President

1969: Pompidou President of France

1969: Unrest over civil rights in Ulster. British army takes over security role

Student Riots
During the 1960s, young people, especially students, were influenced by left-wing and anarchist ideas, and demonstrated for radical political change. In 1968, there were 'student revolts' in London, West Germany, Italy and Holland. In Paris, students fought the police and occupied their universities in May 1968. Backed by striking workers, they paralysed the country for two months.

- ●1965 *Early Bird* communications satellite launched
- ●1965 De Gaulle re-elected President of France
- ●1965 Revolution in Algeria
- ●1966 Indira Gandhi becomes PM of India
- ●1966 England wins soccer World Cup
- ●1966 Coal slurry buries 116 children in Aberfan. Wales
- ●1967 Wreck of *Torrey Canyon* makes oil slick at Lands End. UK
- ●1967 Revolutionary Che Guevara killed in Bolivia
- ●1968 Famine in Biafra shocks world
- ●1968 Civil rights marches by Catholics in Ulster
- ●1968 Papal Encyclical *'Humanae Vitae'* forbids contraceptives for Roman Catholics
- ●1969 Voting age lowered to 18 in UK elections
- ●1969 Edward Kennedy crashes car into River Chappaquiddick
- ●1969 Fighting on border between Russia and China

1969

1970

1970: Tories win election in UK. Edward Heath is Prime Minister

US Moon landings, 1969–72
US astronauts made six landings on the Moon between 1969 and 1972. They travelled across its surface in a moon buggy. Moon landings ceased because they were so expensive.

1971: War between India and Pakistan

Sydney Opera House, 1973
The shell-roofed Opera House is judged one of the wonders of the modern world. Chicago's Sears Tower opened as the world's tallest building in 1973.

Watergate: Nixon resigns

In 1974, Nixon became the first US President to resign, while in office. He did so to avoid impeachment by Congress over his part in the Watergate scandal – this involved a break-in at the (opposition) Democratic Party offices by his aides and the consequent cover-up.

Pakistan and Bangladesh

East Pakistan felt itself neglected by West Pakistan, and in 1971 broke away to form a separate Muslim republic, Bangladesh.

Bangladesh
The new state was very poor and politically unstable. Two of its first leaders were assassinated, Sheik Mujibur Rahman in 1975 and General Zia ur Rahman in 1981.

1971: Idi Amin takes over after military coup in Uganda

1972: SALT 1 (arms limitation talks) signed by US and USSR

Cambodia and the end of the war in Vietnam

Bhutto   Zia

Bhutto and Zia
In Pakistan, Prime Minister Ali Bhutto was ousted in a military coup led by General Zia ul Haq. Bhutto was hanged in 1979, in what was regarded as a judicial murder by Zia.

US troops in Cambodia, 1970
The moderate ruler of Cambodia was overthrown by the Khmer Rouge, who appealed to President Nixon to send US troops to help them fight Communist forces.

1973: UK joins European Common Market

1973: US Vice-President Agnew resigns over tax scandal

Northern Ireland
In Ulster in the early 70s, civil unrest continued and British soldiers were killed by the IRA.

1974: Gerald Ford becomes US President

1974: Labour wins two elections in UK. Harold Wilson becomes Prime Minister

Kent State shootings, Ohio, US, 1970
During renewed protests about US troops in Cambodia and the resumed bombing of N. Vietnam, four students were shot dead by National Guards at Kent State University.

The Vietnam War ends, 1973
The US gradually withdrew its troops. The last left in March 1973 but fighting continued, until the victorious Communist forces took Saigon in April 1975.

Boat people
As Vietnam became a Communist state, many South Vietnamese tried to escape. They sailed in small boats. Many died, but some reached safety and started new lives in the West.

Israel, Jordan and the Palestinians

Palestinian Liberation Organisation (PLO)
Palestinian opposition to Israeli rule was led by the PLO. Their terrorists hijacked airliners and trains and attacked airports, to draw the world's attention to their demands.

Munich Olympics, 1972
Arab 'Black September' terrorists attacked Israeli athletes in the Olympic village. Eleven athletes, five terrorists and a German policeman were killed during the incident.

Yom Kippur War, 1973
War broke out when Egypt and Syria attacked Israel during the religious fast of Yom Kippur. After 19 days of fighting, stalemate was reached and a ceasefire signed.

President Sadat
Prime Minister Begin

The Camp David accords, 1978
Britain and the US sponsored talks between Egypt and Israel. At Camp David, the peace treaty, was signed by Menachem Begin of Israel and Anwar Sadat of Egypt in 1979.

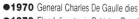

●**1970** General Charles De Gaulle dies
●**1970** Flood disaster in Pakistan/Bangladesh
●**1970** Salvador Allende becomes Marxist president of Chile
●**1970** Native Americans seize Alcatraz prison for 19 months in protest over land rights

●**1971** UK restricts Commonwealth immigration
●**1971** Voting age lowered to 18 in US
●**1971** UK changes to decimal currency
●**1972** Labour wins election in Australia
●**1972** Watergate break-in. Five men arrested

●**1973** President Allende of Chile killed in US backed coup
●**1973** Power cuts cause three-day working week in UK
●**1973** Aborigines granted vote in Australia

●**1974** Emperor Haile Selassie of Ethiopia deposed
●**1974** Democracy restored in Portugal
●**1974** Turkey invades Cyprus: island partitioned by UN
●**1974** President Georges Pompidou of France dies
●**1974** UK anti-terrorist laws passed to fight IRA

Oil crisis

The Arab oil sheiks
In 1973, the Arabs led the organization of oil producers, OPEC, in quadrupling the price of oil and restricting production. This was done because of Western support for Israel.

Queuing for petrol
The resulting shortage of fuel caused petrol rationing and an economic crisis in the West. In Britain, a state of emergency was declared as mineworkers also went on strike.

North Sea oil flows, 1975
The West looked for alternative oil sources within its own control. Britain developed oil fields in the North Sea, and the US built a pipeline to carry Alaskan oil to ice-free ports.

Iran

Shah of Iran flees, 1979
Opposition to the shah's extravagance, autocracy and pro-Western attitudes was expressed in violent demonstrations. These forced the shah to flee into exile in Egypt.

Bloody Sunday, 1972
The British government introduced detention without trial for terrorists. During a protest against this in Londonderry, 13 civilians were shot dead by British troops.

IRA bombing campaign
The IRA began a campaign of terrorist bombings in Ulster and England. They put a bomb in Parliament. Other bombs killed MPs, soldiers, civilians and Lord Mountbatten.

Steve Biko killed, 1977
In South Africa, opposition to apartheid continued with black boycotts of schools. Black rights leader Biko died in police custody, after being beaten and shackled.

Ayatollah Khomeini
Khomeini returned from exile as head of a fundamentalist Islamic Republic. A Revolutionary Council was set up to run the country and democracy was abolished.

1975: Suez Canal re-opened after Egypt-Israeli peace talks

1975: Civil war in Lebanon begins between Christians and Muslims

1975: North Sea oil begins to flow to UK

1976: James Callaghan becomes UK PM. Devalues the pound

1976: Death of Mao Tse-tung

1976: Civil war in Angola

1977: Jimmy Carter becomes US President

1977: Likud Party wins Israeli election. Menachem Begin becomes PM

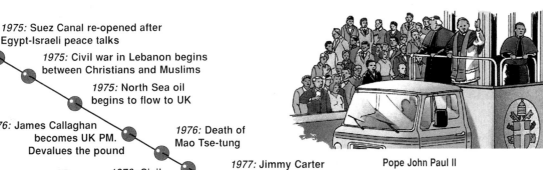

Pope John Paul II
Elected in 1978 after the sudden death of the 'Pope of 100 Days', John Paul I, Polish-born Cardinal Karol Wojtyla was the first non-Italian Pope for 450 years.

1977: Brezhnev takes sole power in USSR

1978: Israel invades Lebanon to strike at PLO camps

1978: PW Botha becomes South African PM

US embassy seige
Support for the new Islamic regime was often expressed as hatred of the United States. When the shah went to the US for medical treatment, militants stormed its embassy in Tehran, and seized 63 Americans as hostages.

King Juan Carlos of Spain, 1975
The Fascist dictator, General Franco, died after ruling Spain for nearly 40 years. The monarchy was restored, and the new king, Juan Carlos, promised to institute reforms.

Concorde, 1976
France and Britain co-operated to build this supersonic airliner, which caused a sonic boom when it broke the sound barrier. It flew between London and New York in 3 hours.

1979: Independence of Zimbabwe (Rhodesia) agreed

1979: Tories win UK election. Margaret Thatcher first UK woman PM

- **1975** Helsinki agreement on human rights signed
- **1975** Communist Khmer Rouge take over Cambodia
- **1975** Mozambique and Angola become independent
- **1975** Communists take over Laos
- **1975** Soviet spacecraft land on Venus and send back TV pictures
- **1976** Egypt ends pact with USSR
- **1976** US bicentennial celebrations
- **1976** First women priests in US and Canada
- **1976** 200 die in Soweto clashes with South African police
- **1977** Queen Elizabeth II's Silver Jubilee
- **1977** UN bans arms sales to S. Africa
- **1978** Sadat and Begin share Nobel Peace Prize
- **1978** Louise Brown, first test tube baby, born in UK
- **1978** Amoco Cadiz shipwreck causes pollution. Brittany
- **1979** Saddam Hussein takes power in Iraq
- **1979** Idi Amin deposed in Uganda

1979

TRANSPORT

Changes in transport during the century have enabled people to travel where they want, quickly and safely. Air transport has opened up the world for business and holidays. The private car is replacing public transport by railway and bus in developed countries, but there is increasing concern about the pollution and congestion the car causes.

US Pacific locomotive, early 1900s
This type of large steam locomotive pulled trains in five continents. In the US a standard model was produced. In other countries, designers like Nigel Gresley (UK) produced modifications of the basic design.

Lusitania
Launched in 1906, Cunard's *Lusitania* was the largest and fastest liner on the luxury transatlantic crossing. It was torpedoed off Ireland by a German submarine in 1915, with the loss of 1,200 lives.

Alcock and Brown, 1919
British Captain John Alcock and American Lieutenant Arthur Brown completed the first Atlantic crossing in a modified Vickers-Vimy biplane. The 3,000 kilometre flight from Newfoundland to Ireland took 16 hours.

1900 First Zeppelin airship flies

1901 First mass-produced motor-car, the Oldsmobile, in US

1901 First Mercedes car built by Daimler in Germany

1903 First Tour de France cycle race held, won by Maurice Garin

1904 First electric trams in UK

1904 Opening of New York subway, US

1904 Rolls and Royce produce first cars together in UK

1905 First motor buses in London

1919 First air passenger service opens, London to Paris

1919 Smith brothers make first flight from UK to Australia

1923 Benz produces trucks with diesel engines in Germany

1928 Malcolm Campbell sets land-speed record of 206 mph (418 km/h)

1934 Moscow subway opens

1935 Speed limit of 30 mph (48 km/h) introduced in urban areas in UK

1937 Frank Whittle builds first static jet engine in UK

1938 Gresley's steam locomotive *Mallard* sets record of 126 mph (202 km/h)

1938 Cunard liner *Queen Elizabeth* launched in UK

1940 First successful flight of helicopter by Sikorsky in US

1947 Supersonic plane in US

1958 First parking meters in London, UK

1959 First Channel crossing by hovercraft, invented in UK

1964 Bullet train in service in Japan between Tokyo and Osaka

1964 Hawker Harrier jump-jet shown at UK air show

1986 Americans Dick Ruran and Jeana Yeager make first non-stop flight around the world

Taxis
In cities round the world, vehicles powered by the internal combustion engine gradually replaced horse-drawn transport. The first motorized taxis appeared on the streets of Los Angeles, in 1915.

Douglas DC3
In 1935, American Airlines introduced the Douglas DC3 passenger aircraft onto its domestic flights. Powered by two Wright Cyclone engines, it had a range of 2,400 kilometres and could carry 21 passengers.

Volkswagen Beetle
In 1936, a factory opened in Saxony to mass-produce the *Volkswagen* or people's car. Designed by Porsche, this small car with a streamlined body was intended to be cheap enough for ordinary Germans to buy.

Hydrofoil, 1950s
Invented by Forlanini of Italy in 1906, the hydrofoil became popular for longer sea crossings in the 1950s. As its foils lifted the hull out of the water, it was faster than the hovercraft, developed by Cockerell in 1955.

Mini car launched in UK, 1959
The Mini, designed by Alec Issigonis, had a revolutionary design, with its engine mounted sideways and its wheels at the four corners. This made it small outside but roomy inside, and easy to manoeuvre in towns.

Jumbo jet, 1970
The Boeing 747 wide-bodied jet, known as a 'Jumbo', carried 362 passengers, twice as many as earlier Boeing models. Its first transatlantic passenger flight went from New York to London, in January 1970.

Mountain bike, 1980s
Cycling became popular again in the 1980s, because of concern over pollution from engine exhausts, and a desire for physical fitness. Mountain bikes had many gears to cope with slopes and rough country, but most were ridden in towns.

TGV in operation, 1981
France's *Train Grande Vitesse* (high speed train) went into operation in 1981. Powered by electricity, it cut the journey time from Paris to Lyons by half. It set the world record for a locomotive of 515 km/h in 1990.

Super ferries, 1990s
During the 1990s, larger ships to carry more pasengers and cars are being built. They provide cheap alternative sea crossings to tunnels like that under the English Channel, opened in 1994, and to air transportation.

ENTERTAINMENT

At the beginning of the century, most entertainment was 'live'. People read books, made music or played games at home; or went out to the theatre, dances, concerts or the music hall, or to watch sport. The Lumière brothers in France developed projectors to show moving pictures early in the first decade, and this became the most popular form of entertainment by the middle of the century. Widespread car ownership from the 1950s onward meant people could travel to theme parks and holiday camps for entertainment and holidays. At the end of the century, television, videos, and portable radios and cassette players brought entertainment back into the home.

78 rpm records, 1901
The first recorded music was played on cylinders, patented in 1900. However, in 1901, flat shellac gramophone records with a spiral groove, playing at 78 revolutions per minute, were introduced into the UK.

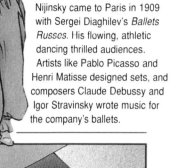

Nijinsky and the Ballets Russes, 1909
The Russian dancer Vaslav Nijinsky came to Paris in 1909 with Sergei Diaghilev's *Ballets Russes*. His flowing, athletic dancing thrilled audiences. Artists like Pablo Picasso and Henri Matisse designed sets, and composers Claude Debussy and Igor Stravinsky wrote music for the company's ballets.

1906 First radio programme broadcast in USA

1920 BBC founded and first regular radio programmes in UK

1927 *The Jazz Singer* the first talking picture released

1927 First demonstration of TV pictures in US

1929 Kodak puts first 16mm cine film on sale

1930s Big band Swing music popular

1936 George Gershwin's folk opera *Porgy and Bess* opens in US

1936 First TV service in UK

1937 First Butlin's Holiday Camp opens in UK

1948 First transistor radios and LP (long playing) records in the US

1951 First colour TV in US

1952 First Cinerama wide-screen films released

1957 Sony put pocket transistor radio on sale

1958 Stereo records on sale

1960 Portable TV built in Japan

1962 *Dr No*, first James Bond film released

1963 Cassette tape recorders on the market

1964 First discothèques opened

1967 *2001 – A Space Odyssey*, a film with spectacular special effects

1970 The Beatles break up

1978 Sony Walkmans on sale

1980s Home computer games widely available

1981 Compact discs (CDs) on sale

1993 Stephen Spielberg's film *Jurassic Park* released

Jazz age, 1920s
Jazz music developed from spirituals and plantation songs, and used African and Latin American rhythms. Until the 1920s it was played only by black musicians. Then it was taken up and adapted by white musicians and big bands. Jazz made stars of black soloists like Louis Armstrong and Ella Fitzgerald.

Penguin Books, 1935
In 1935, publisher Allen Lane brought out a series of cheap paperback books called Penguins. Costing less than a cinema ticket, these brought both novels and non-fiction within the price range of ordinary people.

Charlie Chaplin
British-born Chaplin, with his trade-mark walk, hat and cane stick, was the biggest star of Hollywood comedy films from the 20s to 40s.

Pop music begins with Bill Haley
Rock Around the Clock, by Bill Haley and the Comets, was the first rock-'n'-roll hit song. It topped the pop record charts for five months in 1955. Teenagers danced 'the jive' to the music of pop groups and singers.

Disneyland opens, 1955
The world's first theme park, Disneyland opened in California in July 1955. Covering 64 hectares, it offered fantasy rocket trips to the Moon, a ride on a Mississippi paddle steamer and a mock medieval castle.

Manufactured pop, 1960s
By the 60s, pop music was a major industry. Record producers started new dance crazes, like the Twist, in order to sell more records. Groups like The Monkees were formed to copy the success of The Beatles.

Satellite TV, 1980s
With the launch of communications satellites such as *Telstar* in the 60s, TV pictures could be sent quickly round the world. By the 80s, many homes had satellite dishes, which gave access to a wide range of TV programmes.

Cassettes, CDs and videos
By the 90s, personal stereos, compact discs and mini televisions meant everyone could carry their own personal entertainment with them. With video cassettes, people could watch films at home, as well as in the cinema.

1980

1980: Death of Tito of Yugoslavia

1980: Shipyard strike in Poland

1981: Ronald Reagan becomes US President

1981: Ten IRA prisoners die after hunger strike

1981: SDP formed in Britain

1981: Mitterand President of France

1981: President Sadat of Egypt shot

1983: Thatcher re-elected in UK

1983: US aid for Contras in Nicaragua

1983: Constitution in South Africa gives votes to coloureds

1984: Reagan re-elected

1984: Sikh rebellion in India. Mrs Gandhi assassinated by Sikh guard

1984-5: Miners strike in UK

1985: Gorbachev leader of USSR

1985: Spain re-opens border with Gibraltar

1985: Anglo-Irish agreement on Ulster

1985: Israel withdraws from Lebanon

1986: US planes bomb Libya in response to terrorism

1986: UK privatization of state-owned businesses begins with sale of British Gas

Collapse of Soviet bloc
During the 1980s, the hold of the Soviet Union over its satellite states in Eastern Europe, which President Reagan called "an evil empire", was gradually loosened.

Brezhnev dies, 1982
During the rule of Leonid Brezhnev and his successors Yuri Andropov and Konstantin Chernenko, the USSR continued to oppose moves for democracy in Eastern Europe.

Walesa and Solidarity, 1980–81
In Poland, Lech Walesa led shipyard workers to form a free trades union, called Solidarity. The Russians forced a change of Prime Miinister and Solidarity was banned.

Iran
With widespread popular support, the regime of the ayatollahs restored Muslim law, enforced 'modest' dress for women, and imprisoned and executed its opponents.

War

US attempts rescue of hostages, 1980
A plan to rescue the Tehran embassy hostages using airborne troops failed when their helicopter crashed. This disaster cost US President Carter popular support.

Falklands War, 1982
When Argentina occupied the British Falkland Islands, the UK responded by sending a task-force to reclaim them. After a three-month war, the islands were retaken.

Iranian embassy seige, London
In April 1980, gunmen seized the Iranian embassy in London, demanding the release of political prisoners in Iran. Most were killed when the SAS stormed the building.

Iran-Iraq War, 1980–88
Iraq attacked Iran to try to get control of a strategic port on the Persian Gulf. The war, which caused a million deaths and many casualties, ended in stalemate.

Afghanistan war, 1980-88
The Soviet invasion was condemned by the UN and opposed by Muslim guerillas. The USSR began to withdraw in 1988. In the war, ten thousand of its soldiers were killed.

Lebanon

Israel invades Lebanon, 1982
As Christians and Muslims fought a civil war in Lebanon, PLO terrorists attacked Israel. Israel invaded Lebanon to expel the PLO from their camps around Beirut.

International peacekeeping force, 1982
Christian Falangists entered the camps and massacred civilians after President Gemayel was assassinated. A peace-keeping force of US, Italian and French troops was sent in.

Beirut bombings, 1983
Muslim militiamen opposed the peace-force by suicide bombings, which killed 300 troops in October 1983. They also began to take US and European citizens as hostages.

Colonel Oliver North and 'Irangate', 1987
The US used Oliver North to secure the release of some hostages, by promising arms to Iran. British envoy, Terry Waite, was taken hostage after being involved in these negotiations.

- **1980** Democracy restored in Honduras
- **1980** Robert Mugabe becomes PM of Zimbabwe
- **1980** Michael Foot leader of UK Labour Party
- **1980** Ex-Beatle John Lennon shot dead in New York
- **1980** The West boycotts Moscow Olympics because of Soviet invasion of Afghanistan
- **1981** Inner city riots in Brixton, Toxteth and Moss Side, UK
- **1981** *Voyager 2* sends back pictures of Saturn
- **1981** First London Marathon run
- **1982** Pope John Paul II visits Britain
- **1982** Channel 4 TV begins broadcasts in UK
- **1982** Greenham Common Women's Camp set up to protest against US cruise missiles based in UK
- **1983** Mass IRA escape from Maze Prison, Northern Ireland
- **1983** 'Star Wars' defence programme begins in US
- **1984** IRA bombs Tory Conference in Brighton, UK
- **1984** UK agrees to return Hong Kong to China in 1997
- **1984** Collapse of 70 banks in US

Gorbachev reforms, 1985
When Mikhail Gorbachev became Russian leader, he anounced a policy of *perestroika* (restructuring) and *glasnost* (openness). This prompted reforms in other Communist states.

Year of Freedom, 1989
In 1989, the Communist regimes of Poland, Hungary, Czechoslovakia, East Germany, Bulgaria and Romania fell after popular opposition, and free elections were held.

Berlin Wall comes down, 1989
On November 9th, the East German government removed all restrictions on travel to the West. That same night, the Berlin Wall began to be demolished.

Disaster!

Bhopal, 1984
A leak from a pesticide plant in Bhopal, India, killed 2,000 people. Many more were blinded, or suffered kidney and liver damage. The owners, Union Carbide, promised compensation.

Famine in Africa

Ethiopia and Sudan, 1980s
A combination of drought and disruption caused by civil war brought famines to Ethiopia and Sudan during the 1980s. TV pictures showed the suffering to the world.

Live Aid relief efforts, 1985
Irish singer Bob Geldof formed Band Aid with members of top pop groups to raise money for famine relief. Their records and Live Aid concerts raised millions.

Benazir Bhutto
Daughter of the executed Prime Minister of Pakistan, Ali Bhutto, Benazir took over leadership of his Pakistan People's Party. In the 1980s they protested against the military rule of General Zia. After Zia was killed by a bomb in his plane in 1988, he was succeeded in office by Benazir. Educated at Oxford University, England, she was the first woman leader of a Muslim country.

Chernobyl explosion, April 30, 1986
An explosion at this Soviet nuclear plant sent out a cloud of radioactive gas. The immediate area was evacuated, but some contamination spread thousands of kilometres.

Lockerbie air disaster, 1988
Pan Am flight 103 exploded over Lockerbie, Scotland, after a bomb had been placed in the luggage. It is thought that Libyan terrorists were responsible for the 270 deaths.

Cory Aquino
Ferdinand Marcos, the dictator of the Philippines was overthrown by a revolt of civilians and the army in 1986. He was replaced by Cory Aquino, widow of the opposition leader his agents had killed in 1983.

1987: Thatcher wins UK election

1987: Gorbachev and Reagan sign missile treaty

1987: 'Black Monday' stock markets collapse

1988: Palestinian *Intifada* (resistance) begins in West Bank and Gaza

1988: George Bush elected US President

1988: Military rule in Chile ends after referendum

1989: Death of Emperor Hirohito of Japan

1989: San Francisco earthquake

1989: Vietnamese army leaves Cambodia

1989: Ayatollah Khomeini dies

1989: US invades Panama to arrest President Noriega on drugs charge

1989: FW de Klerk becomes South African President

1989: Pakistan rejoins Commonwealth

Exxon Valdez, 1989
When the supertanker, *Exxon Valdez*, ran aground off the coast of Alaska, a 80km-square oil slick spread out, damaging marine wildlife.

Tiananmen Square massacre, 1989
A student movement for greater democracy in China began with peaceful rallies and hunger strikes. The students occupied Tiananmen Square in Beijing (Peking). The movement was crushed when the army moved into the square with tanks, killing hundreds of young unarmed protestors.

● **1985** Greenpeace ship *Rainbow Warrior* blown up by French agents in New Zealand
● **1985** South Africa ends ban on interracial marriages
● **1985** Bradford football stadium disaster, UK
● **1986** State of emergency declared in South Africa

● **1987** Terry Waite taken hostage in Beirut
● **1987** *Herald of Free Enterprise* ferry disaster at Zeebrugge, Belguim
● **1987** Kings Cross Underground station fire kills 31 people, UK

● **1988** Oil rig *Piper Alpha* explodes in North Sea
● **1988** First Anglican woman Bishop in US
● **1989** In UK, Hillsborough stadium disaster kills 95
● **1989** *Voyager 2* sends back pictures of Neptune
● **1989** Iranian Muslim *fatwah* (death sentence) against novelist Salman Rushdie

1989

INNOVATION

During the twentieth century, advances in the pure sciences, medicine and engineering changed human life in a radical way. The development of rockets and radio telescopes meant humans could see into the far reaches of the universe, and could think about the prospect of travelling to other planets. With electron microscopes and fibre-optic cables they could also see inside their own bodies and detect the tiniest particles of matter. Discoveries in medicine meant many previously fatal diseases were defeated, and there is hope of finding cures for cancer and AIDS. With technological advances, everyday life has become easier for many people. Through television, telephones and computer networks, communication across the world is fast and simple. However, science has also provided the means to destroy the planet with atomic radiation and chemical pollution.

1902 Thomas Edison invents the electric battery

1905 Albert Einstein first writes about his theory of relativity

1907 Lumière brothers develop colour photography process

1910 X-rays first used in a surgical operation

1912 Process to manufacture cellophane discovered

1912 Detection of protons and neutrons in atom

1916 Blood refrigerated and used in transfusions

1918 Size of the Milky Way shown

1919 Ernest Rutherford splits the atom

1921 Marie Stopes opens first birth-control advice clinic in UK

1928 First immunization of humans against tetanus

1929 Iron lung invented in US

1929 Dunlop Co. develops foam rubber

1930 Planet Pluto discovered

1931 Electron microscope made

1941 Beginning of Manhattan Project to develop atomic bomb in US

1942 First electronic computer built in US

1942 Magnetic recording tape invented

1943 Antibiotic streptomycin developed in US

1943 Plastic PVC first used to replace rubber

1946 Radio-carbon dating of objects invented

1948 Modern hard contact lenses developed by Kevin Tuohy as alternative to spectacles

1951 First electric power generated from an atomic power station

1952 First effective vaccine against polio developed

1953 Link between cigarette smoking and lung cancer first shown

1954 First kidney transplant in US

1958 Van Allen radiation belts discovered around the Earth

1966 *Luna 9* spaceship lands on Moon

1967 First pulsar discovered

1974 *Mariner 10* transmits pictures of Mars, Venus and Mercury back to Earth

1980s *Voyager* spacecraft sends pictures of Saturn, Uranus and Neptune

1992 First photo taken of 'Smiley', 'tenth planet' in the Solar System

Gillette safety razor, 1901
US businessman, King Camp Gillette, invented a razor with small, double-edged blades which could be thrown away when they were blunt. The blades were enclosed in a safety holder.

Photocopier, New York, US, 1958
The first photocopy was made by Chester Carlson in 1938, but it was not until 1958 that a commercial machine, using his design of a metal drum with an electrostatic charge to attract toner powder, was marketed by Xerox.

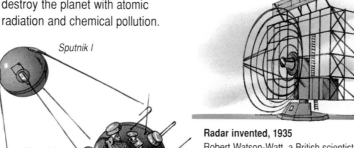

Sputnik I

Vostok I

Radar invented, 1935
Robert Watson-Watt, a British scientist, patented a method of detecting planes and ships by bouncing radio waves off them. By measuring the time the waves took to return, he could calculate how far away they were.

Soviets in space
In 1957, *Sputnik I*, the first satellite, was put into orbit and a month later a dog called Laika was sent into space. *Lunik III*, photographed the far side of the Moon in 1959 and, in 1961, Yuri Gagarin, travelling in *Vostok I*, became the first person in space.

Lasers, 1960
Research into Light Amplification by Stimulated Emission of Radiation (LASER) by Theodore Maiman in the US, led to the manufacture of the first lasers. Their intense beam of pure light could cut through metal.

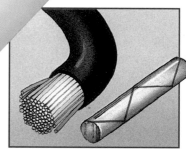

Fibre optics, 1966
Cables made up of optical fibres, strands of pure glass as fine as hair, carry information as pulses of light. They were devised in 1966, and are replacing metal wire for carrying phone and TV communications.

The re-usable space shuttle, 1980s
During the 1980s, the US launched several shuttles – spacecraft which could return to Earth and be used again. The shuttle programme was stopped after *Challenger* exploded on take-off in 1986.

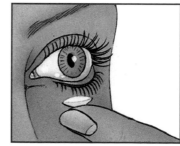

Disposable contact lenses, 1980s
In the 1980s soft contact lenses, which allowed oxygen through to the eye's surface, were invented. Though they were easier to wear than hard lenses, they were also easy to damage.

Mobile phones, 1980s Cellular phones, which uses a two-way radio link rather than wires, became cheaper and smaller in the 1980s. Signals are sent from the phone to a relay station in each area radio cell, and then by landline cables to telephone exchanges. Digital systems, which suffer from less interference than the original analogue systems, came in during the 1990s.

Marconi's wireless, 1901
In 1901, the Italian inventor of the wircless, Guglielmo Marconi, transmitted the letter S in Morse code from Cornwall in the UK to Canada, 3,200km away. This began world-wide communication by radio signals.

Vacuum cleaners
In 1907, the Hoover Company marketed a lightweight household vacuum cleaner in the US. This used an electric motor to suck dirt into a disposable bag, and made housework much easier.

Fleming discovers penicillin, 1928
British scientist Alexander Fleming discovered penicillin, when mould growing on a piece of stale bread in his laboratory killed bacteria it touched. This antibiotic was not manufactured on a large scale until 1943.

Liquid fuel rocket, 1926
US physicist, Robert Goddard launched a rocket powered by gasoline and liquid oxygen.The first rockets remained in the Earth's atmosphere, but Goddard thought they could travel into space.

Biro pens, 1938
These pens, which used quick-drying printers ink in a capilliary tube, and had a ball-point to write with, were invented by Hungarian Lazslo Biro in 1938. After he fled to England to escape the Nazis, he sold the idea to HG Martin, who marketed the pens in 1946, and named them after their inventor.

Nuclear power, 1940s
Enrico Fermi, an Italian physicist working in the US, carried out the first controlled nuclear chain reaction in 1942, using uranium and cadmium rods. The power was then developed for atomic weapons.

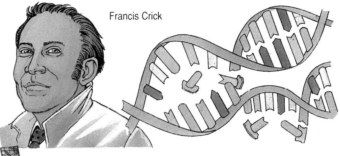

Francis Crick

Crick and Watson discover DNA, 1953
Working in Cambridge, UK, in 1953, Francis Crick and James Watson discovered and modelled the structure of DNA, the material that genes are made of. They showed how the double-helix structure uncoils, locks and recoils to transmit hereditary characteristics in living organisms.

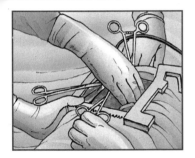

First heart transplant, South Africa, 1967
Working with a team of 30 assistants, Dr Christiaan Barnard transplanted the heart of an accident victim into Louis Washkansky in Cape Town. Advances in surgery and immunology made this operation possible.

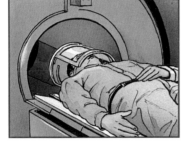

Electronic body scanner, 1979
Briton Geoffrey Hounsfield and American Allan Cormack were awarded the Nobel Prize for Medicine in 1979, for their development of a scanner that produced a complete image of the inside of the body.

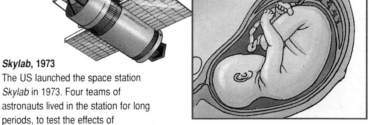

Skylab, 1973
The US launched the space station *Skylab* in 1973. Four teams of astronauts lived in the station for long periods, to test the effects of weightlessness on the human body. They studied weather patterns and the planets, and 'walked' in space to carry out repairs. After 1974, *Skylab* was left empty and it crashed back to Earth in 1979 in the desert of Western Australia.

The first test-tube baby, UK, 1978
Doctors discovered how to fertilize a human egg outside the womb, and in 1978 the first test-tube baby, Louise Brown, was born. Patrick Steptoe and Robert Edwards carried out the treatment that led to her birth.

Micro-surgery, 1980s
Using tiny instruments and television pictures transmitted via slim fibre-optical cables, surgeons were able to operate on delicate tissues within the human body, and even on unborn babies in their mothers' womb.

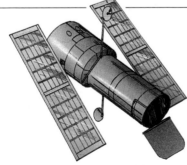

Hubble Space Telescope, 1990
Launched from the space shuttle *Discovery* in April 1990, this telescope was designed to take clearer pictures of the stars and planets than was possible from within the Earth's atmosphere.

Portable satellite terminal, 1990s
Using a small ground station, which is light enough to be carried around, people in places where there are no telephones or fax machines can send messages or data via satellites to anywhere in the world.

Videophone, 1990s
There was a Picturephone network in the US from the early 1960s, but this was very expensive and had poor pictures. Fibre optical cables and digital transmission have made modern models cheaper and better.

1990

1990: **Lebanese militia defeated by Syrians**

1990: **Independence for Namibia**

1990: **EC Maastricht Treaty signed**

1990: **Thatcher replaced by John Major as UK PM**

1990: **West and East Germany reunited under Helmut Kohl**

1991: **Coup and civil war in Somalia**

1991: **Communists overthrown in Ethiopia**

1992: **Military coup in Haiti**

1992: **Democracy restored in Ghana**

1992: **Cory Aquino loses power in Philippines**

1992: **US troops go into Somalia to restore order**

1993: **Single European Market introduced in EC**

1992: **Military coup in Algeria after elections**

1993: **Bill Clinton becomes US President**

1993: **Taiwan recognizes communist China**

1993: **Military coup in Guatemala**

1993: **Eritrea votes for independence from Ethiopia**

1993: **Floods in US Midwest**

1993: **Czechoslovakia splits into Czech and Slovak republics**

1993: **Prince Sihanouk returns to Cambodian throne**

South Africa
Moves towards black majority rule began in 1990, when President de Klerk lifted the ban on the ANC and the Communist Party, and Nelson Mandela was released from prison.

de Klerk Mandela

Mandela and de Klerk
The apartheid laws were repealed in 1991, and de Klerk and Mandela began negotiations about a new constitution. Free elections were held in which all races could vote, and Mandela became the first black president in 1994.

Unrest between ANC and Zulus
Not all black South Africans supported Mandela and the ANC. There were violent clashes in the black townships between ANC supporters and Zulu followers of Chief Buthelezi's Inkatha Freedom Party. South Africa was welcomed back into the Commonwealth and Queen Elizabeth II visited the country in 1995.

Gulf War
In 1990, Iraqi troops invaded Kuwait to take control of its oilfields. The president of Iraq, Saddam Hussein, ignored United Nations demands to withdraw his forces.

Saddam Hussein challenged, 1990
Fearing a further invasion of Saudi Arabia, a multinational force was sent to the Gulf. UN sanctions failed to force Saddam to withdraw his army. He brought British and American workers into Baghdad as hostages to prevent Western air-strikes. Saddam freed the hostages, but refused to leave Kuwait before the January 1991 deadline.

'Desert Storm', 1991
After the deadline expired, British and US planes bombed the city of Baghdad and Iraqi military targets. Iraq fired missiles into Israel and set fire to Kuwaiti oil-fields. In February, Allied tanks stormed into Kuwait and Iraq. After a week of fighting, Kuwait was liberated and the Iraqi army defeated. Saddam remained in power, but tough sanctions forced him to agree to UN inspection of his arms factories.

Kurdish refugees
During the Gulf War, Kurdish guerillas in Northern Iraq rebelled. As Saddam's forces fought them, thousands of refugees were protected in safe havens by UN troops.

Break-up of the USSR
The Baltic states of Latvia, Lithuania and Estonia demanded independence from the USSR. Russian attempts to block independence by force failed and the nationalists won majorities in free elections, held in 1991.

Boris Yeltsin takes over, 1991
An attempted coup by Communist hardliners in Russia was defeated. Gorbachev then resigned and Yeltsin took power. The USSR was dissolved into 15 independent republics.

Rebellion crushed, 1993
The new Commonwealth of Independent States was plagued with ethnic disputes and economic crises. Yeltsin ruled by decree after crushing another attempted hardline coup.

Chechenia, 1994–96
When Chechenia declared its independence from Russia, Yeltsin sent in the army to crush the rebels. The rebels responded by taking hostages from Russian towns and villages.

RUSSIAN FEDERAL SOCIALIST REPUBLIC

Independent states from old USSR
When Latvia, Estonia and Lithuania became independent, they passed laws against Russian speakers. Eduard Shevardnadze became president of independent Georgia.

- ● **1990** UN peace plan for Cambodia
- ● **1990** Rallies in USSR demand democracy
- ● **1990** Poll Tax introduced in England and Wales
- ● **1990** Mary Robinson first woman President of Eire
- ● **1990** West Germany wins soccer World Cup

- ● **1991** Inner city riots in UK cities
- ● **1991** Rajiv Gandhi killed by Tamil terrorists in India
- ● **1991** Poll Tax abandoned in England and Wales
- ● **1991** IRA mortar attack on 10 Downing Street, London
- ● **1991** Aung San Suu Kyi, Burmese democrat, wins Nobel Peace Prize

- ● **1992** Russian President Boris Yeltsin withdraws nuclear missile threat from US and UK
- ● **1992** John Smith becomes UK Labour Party leader
- ● **1992** Yitzhak Rabin becomes PM of Israel, improving prospects for peace with the Arabs
- ● **1992** Australia drops oath of loyalty to Queen
- ● **1992** South African president FW de Klerk given mandate to abolish apartheid

Peace in Israel?

The government of Norway helped with secret talks between Israel and the PLO about peace in Israel and the occupied territories.

Agreement signed, 1993
PLO leader Yasser Arafat and Israeli PM Yitzhak Rabin shook hands after a peace agreement was signed in the US.

Conflict continues
Jewish and Arab extremists tried to upset the peace plan. Suicide bombers on buses killed Israelis. Yitzhak Rabin was shot dead by a Jewish opponent in 1995.

War in Yugoslavia

After the death of Tito in 1980, the presidency rotated between the ethnic groups, but the Yugoslav federation gradually fell apart.

Break-up begins, 1991
Moves by Slovenia and Croatia to leave the federation were opposed by the mainly Serb troops of the Yugoslav government. Bosnia and Herzegovina also declared their independence. War broke out as the various ethnic groups tried to extend the areas under their control. In 1992, the UN sent in troops to secure the airport at Sarajevo, so that relief supplies could be flown into Bosnia.

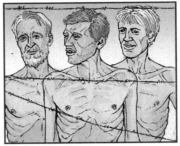

Ethnic cleansing
In 1992, it was revealed that the Serbs were killing, imprisoning and raping members of other ethnic communities, to force them to move out of Serb-held territories.

UN peacekeepers
The United Nations sent in more troops to try to keep the peace and prevent ethnic cleansing, and NATO planes bombed the Serbs. In 1995 a ceasefire was negotiated.

Rwanda

Civil war between the Tutsi and Hutu tribes in the African state of Rwanda broke out again in 1994, after the Hutu president was killed in a plane crash.

Killing fields
The war was marked by slaughter of ordinary members of opposing tribes. The Red Cross estimated 100,000 died in two weeks in May 1994. Many fled as refugees.

Ireland

The IRA called a ceasefire in August 1994 and moves towards peace began to make progress.

Twin-track peace talks, 1995
British and Irish leaders worked on plans for a political settlement for Ulster, while the US-sponsored Mitchell Commission negotiated the surrender of illegal arms by all sides. US President Clinton visited Belfast and heard children talk of their hopes for lasting peace.

1994: Queen Elizabeth and Mitterand open Channel Tunnel
1994: Tony Blair becomes leader of UK Labour Party
1994: National Lottery starts in UK
1994: Russia signs NATO peace accord
1994: US troops restore democracy in Haiti
1995: Terrorist bomb in Oklahoma, US, kills 168
1995: Chirac elected President of France
1995: Communist parties gain seats in Russian elections
1995: French resume nuclear tests in Pacific
1995: Earthquake in Kobe, Japan kills 5,000
1995: Russian assault on Grozny, capital of Chechenia
1995: Earthquake kills 2,000 on Sakhalin Island, Russia
1995: Nolan Committee reports on political sleaze in UK
1995: Nerve gas attack on Tokyo subway
1995: Assassination attempt on Shevardnadze
1996: Israel bombs terrorist bases in Lebanon
1996: IRA end ceasefire with bombs in London, UK

1 Latvia
2 Lithuania
3 Byelorussia
4 Ukraine
5 Moldavia
6 Georgia
7 Armenia
8 Azerbaijan
9 Kazakhstan
10 Uzbekistan
11 Tajikistan
12 Kirgizia
13 Turkmenistan
14 Estonia

The Ukraine controlled many of the former Soviet nuclear installations, and access to the Black Sea. Azerbaijan and Armenia continued fighting over the disputed territory of Nagorno Karabakh.

- **1993** Siege of cult HQ at Waco, Texas, US
- **1993** Australian aborigines given land rights in Native Title Bill
- **1993** Oil spill disaster off Shetland Islands, Scotland
- **1993** Murder of toddler James Bulger by schoolboys shocks UK
- **1993** GATT agreement on worldwide tariff cuts
- **1994** Major earthquake in Los Angeles
- **1994** Ex-US President Nixon dies
- **1994** Women priests ordained in Church of England
- **1994** Queen Elizabeth II visits Russia
- **1994** Brazil wins soccer World Cup
- **1996** Germany wins soccer Euro'96
- **1996** 'Mad Cow' disease brings Europe wide ban on British beef
- **1996** Prince and Princess of Wales divorced
- **1995** Terrorist bomb blast in Oklahoma City, US, kills over 100
- **1995** US football hero OJ Simpson acquitted in murder trial

1999

Personalities of the 20th Century

A selection of a few people whose lives have had an impact on this century.

CLEMENT ATTLEE
(1883–1967)
Prime minister in the post-war UK Labour government, which introduced the Welfare State and National Health Service, and nationalized key industries and utilities.

FIDEL CASTRO
(1927–   )
Cuban revolutionary who established a communist regime in Cuba in 1959 and became its life president.

WINSTON CHURCHILL
(1874–1965)
British prime minister during the World War II, his speeches inspired the British people in their 'darkest hour'.

CASSIUS CLAY
(1942–   )
Heavyweight world champion boxer, whose title was taken away when he refused to fight in the US army. He became a Muslim and changed his name to **Muhammed Ali**.

CHARLES DE GAULLE
(1890–1970)
Leader of the Free French in World War II, he became head of the French Provisional Government 1944–46, and president of the 5th Republic 1958–69. He vetoed the UK's entry into the Common Market.

WALT DISNEY
(1901–1966)
American founder of the entertainment empire that bears his name. His studio began by

making short cartoons (for whose characters Disney provided the voices), then expanded into full length animated features, dramas and nature films, and theme parks.

ALBERT EINSTEIN
(1879–1955)
Physicist whose theory of relativity and equation relating mass and energy led to a new era in atomic physics.

DWIGHT EISENHOWER
(1890–1969)

A relatively unknown US major general, 'Ike' rose to fame as Commander of US forces in Europe in 1942, and co-ordinator of the D-Day invasion. He resigned as NATO's supreme allied commander in Europe to stand as Republican candidate for president. He served two terms as US president between 1953 and 1961. His inauguration was the first to be televized.

HENRY FORD
(1863–1947)
US vehicle manufacturer, whose Ford Motor Company was the first to mass-produce cars on assembly lines. He

was known for his pithy sayings including "History is more or less bunk" and (of his most popular car, the Model T) "You can have it any colour, so long as it's black".

INDIRA GANDHI
(1917–1984)

Daughter of Nehru, the first prime minister of independent India, she shared his political life from an early age, and was imprisoned by the British during World War II. She became leader of the Congress Party and India's first female prime minister in 1966. During her premiership, she survived two attempts to bar her from office for corruption. She was assassinated by her Sikh guards in 1984.

MOHANDAS GANDHI
(1869–1948)
Known as Mahatma or 'Great Soul' by his followers, Gandhi was a lawyer, who led civil rights movements in South Africa and his native India. Because of his religious beliefs, he advocated methods of passive resistance and condemned violence. He was assassinated by a fellow Hindu just after India had achieved independence from the UK.

GEORGE GERSHWIN
(1898–1937)
Beginning as a composer of popular songs, he went on to write opera and classical pieces in jazz style.

ADOLF HITLER
(1889–1945)
Leader of the Nazi Party, and führer (leader) of Germany before and during the World War II. A powerful orator, during the depression he converted large numbers to his fascist and racist views. His legacy lives on in neo-Nazi parties in Europe and the US.

CHIANG KAI SHEK
(**Jianjie Shi**) (1887–1975)
Leader of the Chinese Kuomintang (nationalists) and president of mainland China 1928–31 and 1943–49). After defeat by the Communists, he withdrew to Taiwan and became president of the nationalist Republic of China (1950–75).

HELEN KELLER
(1880–1968)
Having lost her hearing and sight as a baby, she learnt to speak, and went on to obtain a degree. As a social worker, she lectured worldwide on the rights of the disabled.

NELSON MANDELA
(1918–   )
Black South African political leader, he was imprisoned for life in 1964, and became a symbol of opposition to apartheid. He was freed by President De Klerk in 1990, and became president himself after the elections of 1994.

GOLDA MEIR
(1898–1978)
Born in Russia, she became the first woman prime minister of Israel, 1969–74. She led the nation through the Yom Kippur War.

ROBERT MENZIES
(1894–1978)
Prime minister of Australia 1939–41 and 1949–66, he became an elder statesman of the British Commonwealth.

HO CHI MINH
(1890–1969)
Founder of the Viet Minh Communist-Nationalist alliance against the Japanese occupation of Vietnam. He led struggles against the French and US armies after 1945, when he became the first president of the communist Democratic Republic of (North) Vietnam.

JAWALHARLAL NEHRU
(1889–1964)
Elected president of the India National Congress in 1936, he worked with Gandhi for independence. First Prime Minister of independent India, 1947–64.

EMMELINE PANKHURST
(1858–1928)
Founder and leader of the UK radical suffragette

organization, the WSPU. She advocated militant action to secure votes for women and was imprisoned several times. After she encouraged women to do war work during World War I, women's suffrage was won.

DENG XIO PING
(1904–   )
Ageing leader of communist China from 1978, who

liberalized the economy and opened contacts with the West, but also used the army to crush moves for democracy.

POPE JOHN XXIII
(1881–1963)
Born Angelo Roncalli, he was elected Pope in 1958. He called the second Vatican

Council, which began the modernization of the Roman Catholic Church. He broke with tradition by leaving the Vatican to visit prisons and hospitals, and was held in worldwide affection.

YITZAK RABIN
(1922–1995)
First elected Israeli prime minister in 1974, in 1993 he signed a historic peace agreement with the PLO. He was shot by a fellow Israeli at a peace rally.

THEODORE ROOSEVELT
(1858–1919)
US president 1901–09, he was the youngest to hold that office. He won the Nobel Peace Prize for mediating in the Russo-Japanese War.

FRANKLIN ROOSEVELT
(1882–1945)
The only US president to be elected for a fourth term, in his presidency he introduced the 'New Deal' to counter the effects of the Depression, and led the US into World War II.

HAILE SELASSIE
(1892–1975)
Emperor of Ethiopia from 1930, he introduced liberal reforms. Ousted first by the Italians from 1936–41, then by an army coup in 1974.

JAN CHRISTIAAN SMUTS
(1870–1950)
Though he fought against the British in the Boer War, he led South African and UK troops

against German Southwest Africa in World War I and became a British field marshal. An opponent of racial segregation and an advocate of votes for women, he was twice prime minister of South Africa.

JOSEPH STALIN
(1879–1953)
Dictator of the USSR 1924–33, he forced peasants into collective farms and modernized Soviet industry. After his death the extent of his murderous purges was revealed – millions of people had died.

MARIE STOPES
(1880–1958)
English doctor, whose book *Married Love* caused a storm in 1918, she opened the UK's first birth control clinic in 1921, giving free advice.

MOTHER TERESA
(1910–   )
Born Agnes Bejaxhiu in Albania, she went to India in

1928 to teach as a Catholic nun. In 1948, she left the convent to work among the poor and dying of Calcutta, and founded a new order of nuns, the Missionaries of Charity. She was given the Nobel Peace Prize for her work in 1979.

MARGARET THATCHER
(1925–   )
First woman to be prime minister of the UK after the Conservative victory in 1979. Her strong character and distinctive 'Thatcherite' policies earned her the nickname 'The Iron Lady'.

After nearly 12 years in office, she was ousted by members of her own party, and went to the House of Lords as Baroness Thatcher.

MAO TSE-TUNG (Zedong)
(1893–1976)
Revolutionary leader of Communist China from 1949, his Red Book set out the philosophy of the Cultural Revolution of the 1960s.

RUDOLPH VALENTINO
(1895–1926)
First screen star to achieve global fame in silent films of the 1920s, such as *The Sheik*. He was a heart-throb and idol of women of the time. His funeral was a national event in the US.

LECH WALESA
(1943–   )
Polish shipyard worker, who lead the Solidarity trades union in demands for greater democracy in 1980. Imprisoned, he was awarded the 1983 Nobel Peace Prize. He became president of democratic Poland in 1990, but lost power to reformed Communists in 1996.

Glossary

APARTHEID
The Afrikaans word for 'separateness'. Used to describe the system and laws of South Africa which tried to keep races apart – racial segregation.

CIVIL RIGHTS
Citizens' rights and liberties. Most often used to refer to the rights of Black Americans and Irish Catholics

COLD WAR
The period of tension – both military and political – between the United States (and its Western allies) and the Soviet Union, after World War II.

COMMUNISM
A social and political system where the state (the people) own and control the means of production, in order to share more evenly the wealth created by their work.

DEPRESSION
The economic collapse which affected the Western world in the 1930s. People lost money and their jobs, as factories went out of business and prices went up.

DISARMAMENT
The cutting down, or abandonment, of armaments and weapons. Used especially of nuclear arms after World War II and the Cold War.

FASCISM
The extreme right wing philosophy opposed to democracy, which became popular between the two world wars, particularly in Germany, Italy and Spain.

FUNDAMENTALISM
A movement that is based on the strong belief that religious groups must return to the basic teachings of their founders. Used especially of Muslims.

GLASNOST
A Russian word meaning 'being more open and truthful'. Used of Mikhail Gorbachev's policies fom the late 1980s.

HOLOCAUST
The complete destruction of a large number of people. In particular, used to describe the actions of the Nazis against the Jews during World War II.

OPEC (ORGANIZATION OF PETROLEUM EXPORTING COUNTRIES)
The international body, formed in 1960, representing 13 major oil producing states mainly in the Middle East.

PERESTROIKA
Russian for 'doing things in a different way' or 'restructuring' – often used with *glasnost*, above.

TERRORISM
The policy or act of violence or intimidation, often by small revolutionary groups such as the PLO and IRA.

Index